DAVID – SOULMATES

B.J. SMYTH

Happy BBW
Love
B.J. Smyth
x

DAVID – Soulmates

Please note:

This story contains graphic Gay Erotica and is only suitable for Adults 18+

Where can you find me on the Internet
www.facebook.com/BJSmythAuthor
twitter.com/BJSmythAuthor
www.bookbub.com/authors/b-j-smyth

Never miss a new release +follow my Amazon Author page.

Author.to/BJ-Smyth

*T*hrowing the keys on the table as I enter the apartment, slipping off my shoes so I don't get the white carpet dirty, I'm feeling washed-out from the day's work. I may just sit in front of a computer talking to people on the phone—I work in a call centre —but it's still very draining keeping that chirpy, upbeat voice all day. Now it's Friday night, time to hit my local gay bar and see if there is any new talent out tonight.

I look into the mirror on the hall wall and give myself a little smile. "Looking good," I say to myself with a jokey tone to my voice. Walking into my lounge, you can so tell I'm gay; the pristine white room, with artwork of half-naked men on the walls, glass chandelier-style lamps, and a large white leather sofa scattered with bright, colourful cushions. I switch on the CD player and press play. *On a Night Like This* blasts from the speakers as I begin to dance around the room, undoing my tie and throwing it onto the sofa. I break out into a full strip routine, seductively unbuttoning my shirt, revealing my hairy chest and belly as I slip off the shirt, dropping it to the floor. I glimpse myself in the mirror on the wall. I may be overweight, but I still know how to shake my booty.

Still dancing to the music, I undo the belt to my trousers and throw that on the sofa. Now I grind my hips as I undo my trousers, watching myself in the mirror as though I'm doing a strip tease for someone else. My trousers drop to the floor and I step out of them, left with just my tight white work briefs and black socks on as I continue dancing around the room. If my neighbours could see me now, they would be like "Oh my God! Look at him!" but hey, I don't care. Life is too short to worry about what others think.

With two quick skips, I whip off my socks, leaving me enough of the song left to strip off my briefs. My small, fat cock swings as I dance about the room. I may have a small cock but I have nice large balls; well, that's what guys I've slept with tell me.

The next track comes on—*Bad Romance*—as I strut catwalk-style naked to the bathroom. Stepping into the shower, I sing along whilst lathering up my cock as it thickens in my hands; it feels good, but I'm more inter-ested in cleaning my arse. After all, I might get lucky tonight and I want a clean hole for that. I clean and finger myself, getting even more turned on. I'm up for a good fuck tonight. I wonder who will be the lucky man.

I continue cleaning myself; the water on my skin feels wonderful and fresh, like when you've had a stressful day and you step into a rain shower. You cannot beat the feel of raindrops on your skin.

Switching off the shower after about ten minutes, I step onto the bathroom mat and grab a towel to dry off. I look in the mirror. My face has a day of stubble, which gives me an unkempt appearance that looks good on me, so I won't have a shave. I run my fingers through my dark brown hair; it could do with a cut, but will have to do for tonight. I finish drying off, then throw the towel in the washing basket and walk back to my bedroom. Time to decide what to wear; the look is all-important to attract attention in the bar.

Looking through my underwear drawer first, I go for a deep red jockstrap just in case I get lucky. Dark black jeans that hug my arse and a short sleeve, blue, checked shirt complete my lumberjack look.

I stand in front of the full-length mirror and admire my body. I'm a chubby, hairy bear, one nipple pierced with a silver bar, dark black hair all over my body. But the guys I go for like that cute, cuddly look, and I like a well-toned hairy bear guy to fuck me hard. I grab the hair dryer and blow-dry my hair; it's cut short at the sides and long on top so it flops forward to the right side, hanging just above my eyes. Hair dried, I rub gel into it. Next, the aftershave and body spray. Smelling like a perfume counter in a shop, I pull on my jockstrap, adjusting myself into position so it fits over my cock and balls, and outlines my lovely arse.

Putting on the rest of my clothes, I'm ready to hit the town. Walking back into the lounge, *I Feel Love* is now blasting out—a classic, so I will have to listen to this one before heading out. I will get food later; with a bit of luck, someone to share it with as well.

The song finishes, so I swiftly turn off the CD player before I get distracted by another great tune. Heading to the door, I grab my jacket and slip on some shoes. "Time to get that man, babes," I say to myself in the mirror, then give myself a cheeky smile. Grabbing my keys, I head out.

As I walk towards the bar, I can already hear the beat of the music blasting out the windows. There are about seven or eight guys outside and I recognise two of them; Brian and Tony. Getting closer, they notice me.

"Hey, sweetie," Brian calls out with a high-pitched camp voice.

"Hi, babes. How are you?' I reply as I reach them, giving them both a hug and kisses on the cheeks.

"Oh, sweets, I was just telling Tony about this guy I met last weekend. A real husky, hairy guy; fucked me senseless for a good few hours," he screeches out, followed by loud laughter.

"Sounds like my sort of man. Have you seen him again?"

"No, sweets. Another fuck-me-and-leave-me guy, but hey, my arse enjoyed it," he says with another round of laughter.

"You smell good, honey. On the hunt tonight? I can tell," Tony says as he gives me a knowing wink.

"Well, it's been a few weeks since my arse has had any action other than roger, my little bed friend," I say laughing whilst hand-signalling me shoving a dildo up my arse.

"Seems we're all desperate for a good fuck then," Brian screeches.

"Let's hope we're lucky, babes. I must get a drink; my mouth feels like it's been hanging out in a desert all week. Back soon." Taking off my jacket, I throw it over the back of a chair, then walk into the bar, having a quick look around to see if there are any newbies in tonight. I spot a beefy guy sitting in the corner on a tall stool. I haven't seen him before. He glances over at me so I give him a smile, followed by a little lick of my lips. He smiles back at me; you never know, maybe one for later. I carry on to the bar and order a large glass of red, trying to shout over the music as it is so loud.

Just as I pay for the drink and turn around, one of my favourite tracks comes on—*What is Love*. I can't resist a dance to this one so I coolly dance through the crowded pub, making sure I have a quick glimpse at Mr. Beefy in the corner. And, yes, he is watching me as I head back outside to Brian and Tony.

"There is a nice beefcake in the corner inside I've not seen before," I say to Brian.

"Yeah, I spotted him earlier. Waiting to see if he is with someone, sweets."

"We might have a bitch-out then about who gets him," I say with a mixture of laughter and bitchiness.

"Depends what he's into, sweets; a tight, slim arse like mine or fat bubble butt like yours?"

"Ooh, you bitch. Well, if he likes them chunky, he's mine."

We linger outside, watching guys in various shapes and sizes walk into the pub; many of which are just regulars and don't catch my eye anyway. Some others I have already had the pleasure of, or sometimes the not-so-pleasurable times with. I jig around outside to the sounds pumping out of the bar; they play great music here on a Friday night. Having finished my wine, I head back in for another one, hoping Mr. Beefy is still in the corner and alone. I glance over as I walk back in the pub, but he has gone. A wave of disappointment hits me like I have just missed out on the last slice of chocolate cake. Should I have just chatted to him earlier? "Oh, well, his loss," I say to myself.

Ordering another large glass of wine, the music is still playing, shifting into eighties music now; my era, I love eighties music. As I turn to walk back outside, I feel like everything slows down. There in front of me is Mr. Beefy, strutting back past me towards his stool in the corner. I guess he must have been to the toilet. I give him a smile again and he smiles back—lovely white teeth. He has a flawlessly-cut goatee. Walking that close, I can see his hairy chest showing out of the top of his unbuttoned shirt. Close-cropped hair, with a chin carved into perfection. The music breaks my concentration and everything moves in real time again. He heads back into the corner. I look back at him, this time staring a little longer, trying to make eye contact with him. He stares at me and smiles again. I can feel a hot flush overtaking my body as my cock stirs. I'm sure he wants me, but I play it cool and head back outside.

'Mr. Beefcake is so fucking hot. I'm sure he is attracted to me," I say to Brian.

"Sweets, if you want him, you can have him. I have just seen the one I want enter the pub, so we might both be lucky tonight."

"I will give it a few more minutes before introducing one's gorgeous self to him."

Brian laughs. "You knock him dead, sweets."

We both break out into hysterical laughter and dance around outside the pub. A few more guys come along, but none take my fancy like Mr. Beefy has; he is undeniably the one I want tonight. After about another twenty minutes and finishing my wine, I decide it is time to find out more about Mr. Beefy.

"Well, here goes. Wish me luck."

"You don't need luck; just show him your bubble butt, sweets." Brian cackles with laughter again.

I laugh back as I head into the pub, the wine helping to numb my nerves a little.

2

I see him still sitting in the corner on his own, just glancing around the pub. He spots me and gives me another smile. This gives me the courage I need to walk over to him.

"Hi, babes, how are you?" I ask with a slight slur to my voice now that the wine is hitting me.

"Not bad, thanks. How are you?" He has a slight American accent to his voice, which is deep and masculine with a slight gruffness about it. His voice alone sends shivers down my spine. This close to him, I can see he has deep brown eyes; the colour I love.

"Having a nice evening so far. Are you waiting for someone?" I cannot believe I came out and said it.

"No one in particular; just felt like a drink this evening."

I feel like saying *well, you've found him, let's go*, but hold back on that.

"Do you mind if I sit with you?" I ask with a smile and a little giggle.

"Not at all. Take a seat."

I clamber onto a stool next to him, leaning in closer so I can hear him over the music. I can smell his woody, spicy aftershave. I love that manly smell; it reminds me of my gym teacher at school. I always had a crush on him.

"I have never seen you in here before, babes."

"My first time. I have walked past many times but never come inside."

I wouldn't mind you coming inside me, I hear the voice in my head say. I don't say it out loud. He is even more handsome up close.

"You don't have a drink; would you like one?" he asks me. I can feel his breath on my face as he leans closer into me.

"Oh, babes, I never came over here to get you to buy me a drink."

"I'm sure you didn't, but I would like to buy you a drink. What would you like?"

"If you insist, I will have a glass of red then, thank you."

His leg brushes against mine as he gets off his stool and I feel my face glow a little.

"Back in a min," he says with a little wink at me.

This must be my lucky night; not only is this guy great-looking with a real deep, sexy voice, he must be interested in me as he is buying me a drink. A few minutes later, he reappears, carrying two glasses of wine.

"Here you are, sweetheart," he says. As he passes me the glass, my fingers brush against his as I take it into my hand. I blush again. Why am I feeling so giddy? I'm acting like a kid in a candy store.

"So, do you come in here often then?" he asks as he settles on his stool.

"I've been in here more times than I can remember; it's my local bar."

"I almost forgot. What's your name?" he asks.

"David. What's yours?"

"I'm Bradley," he replies, holding his hand out for me. He grips my hand firmly and shakes. It's rare I shake someone's hand in a gay bar; usually I'm so drunk I lunge in for a kiss. Bradley seems different from other guys I typically meet; there is something kind of masterful about his presence.

"Cheers," he says, raising his glass. We clink our glasses together and settle into a conversation about the pub and the music playing. It seems we both like eighties music a lot, so I assume he is about the same age as me. As the conversation flows, he brushes his leg against mine. I'm not sure if it is intentional or by accident, but I'm not complaining.

I'm conscious the wine is making me slur even more whilst we chat away. Then, without warning, he stands up, leans forward, and kisses me; just a little peck on the lips.

"I need to use the little boys' room," he says then walks away.

Wow. I sit, gobsmacked. He does like me. My cock stirs again, but more than that, I get a nice tingling feeling in my arse as thoughts of him pounding into me flood my mind. I want to run outside and tell Brian, but

I decide it would be better to stay here until he comes back.

Minutes later, he is back.

"You didn't run away then," he says with a little laugh.

"I wouldn't run from you. You can kiss me anytime." As the words leave my mouth, he leans forward and kisses me again, this time lingering. I feel his hand on the back of my head as his tongue pushes into my mouth, exploring deep inside, playing with my tongue. After a while he lets go. Looking me in the eyes, he gives me big smile. "You're gorgeous," he says.

I cannot believe my luck. This handsome guy is telling me I'm gorgeous; he is fucking hot, hot, hot. "You're a good kisser," is all I can say.

"Thanks, you're all right yourself."

He sits and stares at me. His eyes burn into mine, and although I feel awkward, I cannot look away.

"Do you want to go somewhere for something to eat?"

I want to eat him, but I can't say. "Yeah, but I need to visit the little girls' room," I say, giggling as I try to get off the stool without stumbling. This wine has certainly gone to my head.

"Okay," he replies.

When I get back, he has already put his jacket on and finished his wine. So I down the last of mine. He gives me one more long, lingering kiss. This time his hands grab my arse cheeks and pull me into him. I'm sure I can feel his hard cock pressing against me before he lets me go.

"My jacket is outside with some friends. I will pick it up on the way out," I say, catching my breath.

We head outside to where Brian is still chatting with Tony.

"Hey, sweets, who is this you've picked up?" he asks, sounding drunk.

"This is Bradley. We're off to get something to eat, babes."

"Oh, I bet you are, cheeky bitch. Don't do anything I wouldn't," he screeches and laughs.

"Catch you soon." I give Brian two kisses and grab my jacket off the chair, then head along the street with Bradley. I'm tempted to hold his hand, but I don't know how he would react.

We only walk a short distance from the pub when Bradley stops walking outside a posh looking restaurant.

"This place will do," he says, gesturing for me to enter.

We step inside the entrance and are greeted by a man wearing a black suit and crisp white shirt.

"May I help you, gentlemen?" he asks with a very elegant English accent.

"Could we have a table for two please in the Crypt? We have not booked," Bradley says.

"Yes, sir, please follow me."

We follow the man down winding stone steps to the left of the entrance. I'm wondering what this Crypt place is like. As the man opens a door at the bottom of the stairs, we're surrounded by the sound of music. I recognise the song, but it is just instrumental; a piano and cello playing *Say Something.* I love the song, but it reminds me of my ex.

The restaurant is amazing. Black and white art deco pictures line the room; it feels like we have stepped back in time to the 1920s. There are only about eight small tables set for two diners each in the place. Just over to the right side, there is a small stage where a pianist and cellist are playing the music. This is a real posh place. I dread to think how much the food in here will cost, but we are here now I will look like an idiot if I suggest we go somewhere else.

The man hands us over to a waiter who escorts us over to a table in the corner where we both take our seats. He hands us both a menu.

"Can I get you drinks whilst you decide on the menu?"

Before I can speak, Bradley replies, "Yes, please. Could we have a bottle of pink Prosecco on ice."

"Certainly, sir," the waiter then hurries away and through another small door to the side.

Bradley smiles at me, then reads the menu. I look down at the menu and I was right; it is very expensive. This man clearly has expensive taste. I browse the menu, looking for the cheapest food I can order.

"Are you having a starter?" Bradley asks.

"I'm not sure. Are you, babes?"

"What do you fancy for the main course? Then maybe we could share a starter; oh, and this meal is on me," he says giving me another flash of his perfect white teeth.

"Don't be silly. I have only just met you. I can pay

14

half," I say, hoping he insists on paying it all as it is so expensive.

"No, it was my choice of restaurant so the meal is on me. Please order anything you like."

"Okay, if you are sure."

"Unquestionably. It's my pleasure."

I look back at the menu, this time looking for something I fancy to eat regardless of price, deciding on a salmon dish that sounds lovely. I sneak little glances at Bradley when I think he is not looking. He is a handsome guy, his shirt open just enough to show his thick, dark, hairy chest.

The waiter reappears with the Prosecco and pours a small amount into my glass, then waits. Why he picked me to taste it I don't know. I haven't got a clue about wines. I don't want to show myself up so I take a sip from my glass and it tastes amazing, so I give a little nod of approval. The waiter fills both our glasses, then puts the bottle into an ice bucket at the side of the table.

"Are you ready to order?"

We both tell the waiter what we would like, which he scribbles into a little pad before whisking away. The soothing music is still playing in the background.

"I'm so pleased you came over to talk," Bradley says in a soothing voice.

"Well, you're so good-looking, babes. I was amazed you were interested in me."

"I noticed you the minute you walked into the bar tonight. I don't ordinarily pick guys up in bars, to be honest."

"Well, it's both our lucky night then."

We carry on the small talk for a while, then the waiter returns with our main courses; we skipped a starter because I had fish and he had meat. He refills our glasses, then leaves as fast as he arrived. The food is amazing; it may be expensive but as they say, you get what you pay for. They play another song I love —*Flashlight*.

"This place is lovely, babes."

"I'm glad you like it."

"The food is great, and this background music is sending shivers down my spine. I've never been to such a nice place."

"You deserve the best," he replies, making me giggle with embarrassment.

We both finish eating our main courses.

"Would you like a dessert?"

"I'm not sure I should, babes. I need to lose a bit of weight."

"Nonsense, you are gorgeous as you are."

I feel my face burn as I smile at his comment.

"You're such a smooth talker," I say with a giggle; the mixture of red wine and Prosecco is making me feel very drunk now.

"So, dessert?"

"Just you will do, babes." The words leave my mouth before I can stop them.

"Now who is being cheeky?" He laughs at me. "Shall I get the bill then?"

"Okay, thank you again for a lovely meal."

"It was my pleasure."

Bradley pays the bill, then we both head out of the

restaurant. Stepping out into the fresh air, the alcohol hits me again and I get dizzy. Bradley grabs my arm.

"Careful there, we best get you home."

"Your home or mine?" I ask, still giggling.

"Mine, if you're up for some fun," he says in his deep, sexy voice.

"Show me the way, babes." I hold onto Bradley's arm as he helps me walk down the road. It doesn't take long for us to reach his house.

3

*F*eeling drunk now, I pay little attention to the outside of the house and hold onto the wall as Bradley opens the front door. He gestures for me to go inside. I step inside onto a white marble floor in a large entrance hall. The walls are all white with small pictures hanging sparingly around them.

"Would you like a coffee?" Bradley asks.

"Yes, please. Black, no sugar."

"Let me take your jacket. Make yourself comfortable in the lounge." He points to a door on the right, then walks towards a door at the end of the entrance hall carrying my jacket.

I open the door. The marble floors continue into the room; another clinical room with minimal furniture. There is a large, ornate fireplace with a beautiful picture of a man looking out to sea from the cliffs hanging above it. I slump down onto the large black leather sofa and stare around the room. The one thing I notice is that there is no TV in the room.

Bradley comes into the room and hands me a cup of coffee before sitting down next to me.

"Your place is beautiful, babes."

"Thanks, I have been here about two years now. It took a while to get it how I wanted it."

I gulp the coffee. It is strong; definitely not instant coffee but just what I need to liven me up.

"It is a lot bigger than my apartment. Do you live here alone?"

"Yes, I moved here after I split from my last relationship."

We chatter away for a while, making small talk whilst I drink my coffee. As the coffee kicks in, I put my cup down and lean into Bradley, placing my lips on his. He kisses me back, rapidly taking control. His strong hands hold me as he softly bites my lips. His tongue slips in and out of my mouth.

He breaks away. "Come with me." He stands and pulls me off the sofa. Holding my hand, he leads me through the entrance hall to another door at the end on the right. He opens the door and there are stairs leading down to a basement room.

"I want you," he whispers into my ear then walks down the stairs. I follow him down.

The room has black marble floors and deep red flock wallpaper on the walls, a large bed draped in red and black silk to one side. What grabs my attention is the sex swing in the corner the room, surrounded with mirrored walls and ceiling.

I hear a very slow, sexy version of *Umbrella* play in the background.

He leads me over to the bed, kissing me again. I feel his hands undoing my shirt. I don't resist. I want him to fuck me. He removes my shirt and pulls me into his arms, his hands sliding over my back as his tongue explores my mouth, then he gently bites down my neck. sending shivers down my spine.

"You're gorgeous," he says in a low, gruff voice.

He gets down on his knees in front of me, undoing my belt and jeans. He pulls them to the floor, revealing my hard cock stretching against my tight jockstrap.

"Very nice," I hear him mumble, feeling his face press against my cock as he breathes intensely then bites the head of my cock through the material of my jock.

I want him to throw me on the bed now and fuck my arse hard, but he continues his slow seduction, pulling my jock down. He stands up and kisses me. "Sit down on the bed." I do as he says without question, my cock hard and wet. He gets back on his knees and lifts my feet out of my jeans and pants, not removing my socks. I feel his mouth bite my toes through the material and breathe deeply against the soles of my feet.

He stands again and I watch him as he removes his own shirt, his skin dark, tanned like a Greek god; thick, black hair on his defined chest, his abs sculpted like a bronze statue. My heart is beating faster as he undoes his jeans. I'm gagging for him and want to see his cock.

His jeans fall to the floor, revealing tight white briefs, his own cock stretching the front of them. He pulls them down, releasing his cock and balls. As he stands, I see his full, hard cock; it's at least eight inches and cut.

The music changes in the background as he tells me

to shift up the bed then climbs on top of me. His cock slides against mine as he lowers himself and bites my nipples. I'm lost in the ecstasy of his mouth biting me and tugging at my nipple bar, his cock thrusting against me, and the music—hot and sexy, hitting my senses—as I smell his manly aftershave.

He slides down my body, nibbling at my skin as he does. He reaches the head of my cock, licking around the inside of my foreskin, then kissing my cock as he moves down to my balls, softly sucking them into his mouth. Then he pushes my legs up in the air as his wet tongue licks around my hole.

Fuck, I want his cock inside me now; all eight inches. He continues rimming me; my arse gapes as he pushes his tongue into me. He climbs back up the bed, pushing my knees back towards my chest. I know what's coming. The head of his cock pushes against my hole lightly just twice, then he rams his full length into me, his thick cock stretching my hole.

I yell out, but he holds his cock deep inside me and lowers himself on top of me, kissing me. "Relax," he whispers in between kisses. Then he pulls his cock fully out of me and rams it deep into me again, thrusting in and out of me, my cock hard and leaking pre-cum as his cock rubs against my prostate. I moan noisily as he fucks me hard, pushing my knees further back, giving him more access to my arse. He continues fucking me. His thrusts get faster, sweat dripping from his head and chest. He grunts with every thrust. With one last deep push into me, I feel his cock throbbing inside me as he roars out, his cum shooting deep into me. I grab my own hard cock and rub it fast; thick cum shoots over my belly and chest. Bradley collapses onto me, his body sticking to mine with the mix of sweat and cum.

"That was fucking good," he says in between deep breaths.

"Sure was, babes."

Bradley lays on my chest, catching his breath. I wrap my arms around him, holding him tight. After a while, he shifts to my side. The cool air hits my wet, sticky chest and belly. Bradley snuggles into me and drifts off to sleep. I must have fallen asleep as well, until I am woken by the feel of someone stroking my cock. I look at Bradley. "Ready for more, gorgeous?" he asks.

"All yours," is the only reply I give.

Bradley rolls me over so I'm face down on the bed. I feel him climb on top of me, his cock rubbing against my arse as his hands hold onto my shoulders. A few thrusts and he is deep inside me again; his cock as hard as before. I moan with pleasure as he fucks me. I feel his chest hair rub onto my back as he begins softly biting the side of my neck, his cock thrusting faster and deeper into me.

"You have a nice tight arse," he growls into my ear, his breath getting heavy again.

"Fuck me hard."

He doesn't need any encouragement. With deeper thrusts, his balls slap against my arse before he shoots his load into me. He is breathless and sweating, just laying on top of me, his cock still having little spams inside me.

After a while, he rolls off me, laying on his back beside me so I snuggle up against him, resting my head on his chest, and we both drift off to sleep again. It's been a long time since I got fucked twice in one night.

I'm abruptly woken by my phone message tone ringing somewhere in the room. Laying on my own in the bed, I take a while to gather my thoughts and remember where I am. I wonder where Bradley has gone. There is just enough light in the room to see, glowing from a small lamp in the corner of the room. I hear footsteps coming down the stairs.

"Morning, gorgeous, did you sleep well?"

"Yes, thanks, babes."

"I'm just making breakfast. If you want to have a shower, it's through that door. Come upstairs once you're ready."

He turns and runs back up the stairs. I lay there for a while, looking around the room, still intrigued by the sex swing in the corner. I wonder how many guys he has fucked on that. After a while, I get up and head into the shower, getting my clothes back on. I check my phone. There is a message from Brian asking how the night went, so I send a reply "*All good chat later x*".

Walking up the stairs, I can hear music playing and Bradley singing along. I follow the sound and find him in the kitchen; the table in the corner is arranged for two.

"Hey, grab a seat. I cooked you a full English breakfast. I hope it's not too much?"

"That's lovely. You didn't need to, though," I reply, sitting at the table.

"I thought you deserved it after last night."

"Thanks."

Bradley joins me at the table with the breakfast and we eat in silence. *Lovely Day* is playing on the radio; an appropriate song for how I'm feeling today. After I finish my breakfast, I break the silence. "I had a wonderful night last night. Thanks."

"So did I. All being well, we can do it again another time," Bradley replies.

"I would love that. Would you like my number?"

"Yes, please."

I'm gobsmacked that this hunk of a guy wants to see me again. Usually, men wake up the morning after at my place, realise they have fucked a fat guy, and can't wait to get out of my apartment.

We exchange phone numbers. "I better head off as I have things to do today," I say, making an excuse to leave so I don't outstay my welcome.

"Okay, David. Catch up soon," he says with a smile.

I'm surprised he remembers my name. Bradley shows me to the door, handing me my jacket and giving me a quick kiss just before he opens the door.

"Take care," he says.

"You too."

Those are the last words I say to Bradley as I leave the house and he closes the door. I recognise the street once I'm outside and take a slow walk home. What a great night out.

4

*I*t has been a week now since our meet and I've not heard from him until this afternoon, when I received a text message—

Hey, David, was wondering if you fancied a meal at mine tonight?

—sending shivers of excitement through my body, putting me on a high all afternoon. This handsome man wants me to go to his place tonight. The memories of last Friday flooded back into my mind; his gorgeous, tanned, hairy, ripped daddy-body, sculpted like the statue David but with a much larger cock, the drips of sweat running down his chest, glistening from the light in the corner of the room as he fucked me face-up on the bed.

Without hesitation, I sent a message back.

Yeah, for sure what time? x

He replied:

Let's say about 7pm, do you remember my address?

How could I forget his address? The memories of

that night and the morning after are imprinted onto my brain. I reply to his message swiftly, as if he would change his mind.

Yeah, no worries see you then x

I then begin clock-watching, as I want to get home and make sure I look my best for tonight. Like always, when you want time to fly, it seems to drag. Eventually, five p.m. arrives and I hurriedly shut down my computer.

"Got to run, girls, I have a hot date tonight," I shout out to my colleagues in an excited tone.

Two girls whistle at me and Mandy shouts out, "I hope you will be a good boy?"

"Nah, babes, I need to be extremely naughty so he gives me a good spanking," I screech out and laugh.

Most of them laugh back, apart from the stuffy ones that don't know how to have a laugh. They give me dirty looks, not that I care.

"Well, don't come in here Monday telling us you can't sit down," Mandy says with a wicked laugh; she loves to play along with me.

"Okay, laters." I rush out the door before she can reply, as I don't have long to get home and change. I live within walking distance of work, so I skip along merrily back to my apartment.

Walking into the apartment, it's about 5:30 p.m. and my thoughts turn to what to wear for the evening, although I hope I'm not wearing my clothes that long. I still want to try out the sex swing. My cock stiffens as I imagine Bradley fucking me in it. I dash into the bathroom and undress, throwing my clothes into the washing basket. Turning on the shower, I step under the steaming water. The water cascades against my chubby body as I turn around, getting myself wet.

Stopping with my back to the shower I lather up, my hands sliding over my hairy chest and belly, my cock semi-erect. Making sure I clean myself well, spending a while in the shower, paying particular attention to my cock, balls, and arse, as I am hoping Bradley will taste them later. Once I'm nice and clean, I rinse off and switch off the shower, stepping out into the bathroom, grabbing a towel and drying myself. I walk into the lounge and switch on the CD player. *What's My Name* blasts from the speakers and I start to dance around the room.

I live alone so need not worry about anyone walking in on me naked, the one good thing about having your own apartment; you can sit around naked whenever you want.

I dance about, breaking into a sexy routine as I watch myself in the mirror, my small cock flapping around as I bounce about the room. The song ends and *All The Lovers* plays, so I head off to the bedroom to pick my clothes and get dressed. I remember Bradley liked my red jock last time, so I rummage through my under-wear, looking for a nice jockstrap to wear. Slipping on the jock, black with a red trim, I adjust my cock and balls into place, then walk over to the wardrobe and pick a pair of jeans and a pink shirt, which I put on, leaving the shirt untucked.

I spray myself with aftershave, deciding to just let my hair dry naturally. By the time I walk to his place, it should be almost dry. Walking back into the lounge I turn off the CD player. Checking the time—its 6:20 p.m.—it should take me about thirty minutes to walk to Bradley's place. I don't want to be late, so I slip on my shoes, grab my phone, wallet, and keys, then head out. Taking a slow walk to Bradley's, as I wouldn't want to arrive sweating like a pig, I arrive about 6:55 p.m. and ring the doorbell.

Bradley opens the door, looking as handsome as I remember. He is wearing black trousers and a crisp white shirt, the first two buttons undone, revealing his hairy, tanned chest.

"Good evening, sexy. Nice and prompt, I see," he says with a big smile, showing his perfect, white teeth, glowing against his tanned face. I remember how deep and sexy his voice is and how it turns me on.

"Evening, babes, nice to see you again," I reply, blushing as the last time we met I was awfully drunk.

"Come in. Can I take your jacket?" He stands to the side and gestures me into the house. As I walk into the large hallway, he closes the door behind me. I slip off my jacket and hand it to him.

"You're looking lovely tonight," he says, then leans forward and places a gentle kiss on my lips, his soft touch sending my heart fluttering. The smell of his after-shave hits my senses; a deep wood and spice smell reminding me of last Friday. I want to grab hold of him and rip his clothes off, but I'm here for dinner so I try to stay cool.

"Please take a seat in the lounge." He points to the room on my right where we had coffee last Friday night.

I walk into the lounge and sit on his luxury sofa. In a few minutes, he comes back into the room, carrying a bottle of pink Prosecco and two glasses. Sitting next to me, he hands me an empty glass.

"I took the liberty of getting the same as last Friday because you seemed to enjoy it in the restaurant."

"Yes, it was lovely."

He smiles at me as he pours the Prosecco into my glass.

"Dinner will be ready in about ten minutes."

"No rush. It's nice to be here."

"Cheers," he says as we clink our glasses together, then I sip the Prosecco.

"Lovely and nice, as I remember."

"I'm glad. Would you like any music?"

"Something nice and soothing would be good, babes."

"Play relaxing selection," he says in his deepest sexy voice. Music plays. I try not to look shocked, but I am impressed; he must have a voice-activated system.

"I'll check how dinner is coming along. Make yourself comfortable."

I cannot believe I'm sitting in this lovely house with this handsome guy cooking me a meal, I'm never usually this lucky. Bradley appears back at the door.

"Dinner is ready. Would you like to follow me?"

Clambering off the big, comfy sofa whilst clutching my glass, I get up and follow him into the room next door. I stare at his backside, hugged by his tight-fitting black trousers. The same music is playing quietly in the background and I have to hold back from letting out a "wow" at the sight of the dining room.

In the middle of the room is a large eight-seater dining table, with black leather high-back chairs around it. A crisp white tablecloth covers the table, and at one end, two places are set with expensive-looking cutlery, a single candle burning between the two settings.

"Please sit; the choice of chairs is yours."

"Thanks. This looks lovely; I can't wait for the food."

Then Bradley sits down opposite me, shakes his napkin and places it on his lap. I pick up my napkin and place it on my lap, then smile at Bradley.

To my surprise, a man dressed in chef whites walks into the room carrying two plates of food. Without speaking, he places the plates down in front of us. He looks familiar to me but I can't quite place where I have seen him before.

"I hope you enjoy. Please ring when you have finished," he says, pointing to a small bell on the table that I had not noticed.

"Thank you, Richard," Bradley says.

I must have had a shocked look on my face.

"Are you okay?"

"Yes, babes, I wasn't expecting someone else to be in the house, and for them to bring the food out."

"I'm not the best cook, to be honest, so I thought it would be better to get a professional in for the night. Don't worry. Once the meal is over, he will leave."

That thought isn't even on my mind. I'm wondering how wealthy this guy is that he can afford professional cooks at home. I look down at my plate. The food looks like it's from a high-end restaurant; scallops drizzled with a dark sauce.

"Well, the food looks lovely."

"I'm pleased. Richard is a chef from the Crypt restaurant."

"Oh, I thought I had seen him before; that explains it."

We both eat the first course, then after a while, Bradley rings the little bell on the table. Richard comes back into the room, collects the plates, then disappears into the kitchen, returning with more plates of food. He places them on the table and leaves again without a word.

The main course was the same dish I had in the restaurant the first night we met. I look up at Bradley and give him an approving smile.

"Well, eat up then," he says.

Without hesitation, I begin eating; there is very little conversation whilst we eat. Once we have both cleared our plates, Bradley refills my glass and then stares at me with his gorgeous eyes as I feel his foot rub against my leg.

"I hope the meal meets your requirements."

"Babes, it's all been lovely so far. Richard is a superb cook."

"He is. Shall we see what he has prepared for dessert?"

"Yes, I'm sure it will be wonderful."

Bradley rings the little bell again, and, as before, Richard comes in the room, clears the plates, then returns with dessert; a selection of three mini gateau-style cakes, elegantly dribbled with a sweet caramel sauce.

"This looks mouth-watering."

"It does indeed. Enjoy." We both eat the dessert.

The time must have flown by. When I look at my watch, it's already 9:15. We finish our desserts, then Bradley rings the bell one final time and Richard appears to clear away the plates.

"Would you like any coffee?" Richard asks.

Bradley looks at me, waiting for me to answer.

"Yes, please. Coffee would be great, and the meal was fantastic, Richard. You're a wonderful cook."

"Thank you, sir."

I am surprised he is so formal, but I say nothing. Bradley also asks for coffee. Richard seems to only be away minutes, and then he's back with two Irish coffees, which he places on the table.

"If that is all for the evening, I will head off. If that's okay, sir?" Richard asks Bradley.

"Yes. Thank you, Richard."

Richard leaves the room, then a few minutes later I hear the front door open and close.

"We have the place to ourselves now," Bradley says.

I feel more relaxed knowing we are alone in the house.

"Well, the meal and evening has been wonderful, babes."

"Hopefully the evening is not over yet."

"Do you have something else in mind then?" I ask

with a slight giggle, hoping we would get to his sex room.

Without a word, Bradley stands up and walks to my side. He leans down and places a gentle kiss on my lips. "Come with me," he says, flashing his lovely white teeth at me.

At once, I stand up and follow him. There's something very commanding about Bradley, even though he can be so gentle. We walk from the dining room to the door that leads to his sex room. He stops outside the door and pulls a key out of his pocket, holding it out in the palm of his hand.

"If you take this key and open the door, you're giving me permission to do whatever I please to you," he says in a deep, sexy voice.

I gulp as the thoughts of him fucking me hard on the swing fly through my mind. My heart racing fast, my hands sweating, I can feel the hairs on the back of my neck standing. I look deep into his eyes.

"I'm all yours." My voice is shaky from the excitement building within me as I reach for the key and open the door.

5

*B*radley follows me down the stairs. The room is just as I remember it; a soft, ambient glow from the light in the corner, the slow, erotic music playing in the room. Bradley grabs my hand and leads me to stand in front of the bed, turning me to face him.

"Stand here," he says, then walks to the corner where the sex sling is hanging on a frame. He pulls open one drawer in a cabinet near the swing. I cannot see what he takes out of the drawer, but he walks back over to where I am standing. He has a red silk scarf in his hands, which he folds to create a blindfold and ties over my eyes.

"This will heighten your senses," he whispers into my ear. I can feel his breath on my skin, not knowing if he is in front or behind me. I feel his hand brush tenderly along my jawline, then trace down my neck, his fingers stopping within the open neckline of my shirt, pressing against my chest.

He begins to slowly unbutton my shirt. Shivers run

down my spine as I feel his wet tongue circle my right nipple, making it stiffen. His tongue then moves to my left nipple, making that one stiffen. He then removes my shirt from my shoulders and pulls it off my arms. I'm now standing, blindfolded, in only my jeans. He runs his fingers up my spine with soft, gentle touches. My mouth is now watering, my cock hard in my jock. I want him to just rip off my clothes and fuck me, but he doesn't. I feel a tug at my belt as he releases it, then unbuttons my jeans and pulls them to the floor.

His hands slide up the inside of my legs to the top of my inner thighs, then slide around the back and over my arse. I feel his mouth kiss my cock through the material of my jock, making it throb. I'm already leaking pre-cum.

Then his hands vanish. I can't feel him near me or hear him moving around in the room. I seem to stand for ages.

"Bradley, are you still here?"

"Don't speak," he growls loudly at me, sounding annoyed.

I say nothing else. Minutes later, I feel the hair of his chest against my back, his cock pushing against my arse as his fingers grip my nipples tight. He kisses and bites my neck.

My body is tingling all over as he kisses down my spine. His hands grab my arse cheeks and pull them apart as his tongue, wet and juicy, licks between them, searching out my hole. I try to move my legs further apart but they are restricted by my jeans around my ankles.

His tongue circles my hole, pushing into me now and then, making me push back against his face. Then, without warning, his tongue disappears and I feel a searing pain on my arse as his hand slaps it hard. I want to call out in pain but I don't want him to shout at me again. I gave him permission to do what he wanted by opening the door.

His hands grab the sides of my jock and pull it down, causing my hard cock to bounce back, hitting my belly. There is nothing gentle about his actions now. I feel his fingers trace along my belly, brushing through my pubic hair. They slide down the shaft of my cock, then grip firmly around my balls, pulling them down away from my body. Pain shoots through them as he tightens his grip. Just as I'm about to call out, he releases them and I feel his tongue lick the tip of my cock.

He is playing with me, taking me from pain to pleasure, like he is testing my endurance.

A few more licks, then he stops again. He is teasing me, my cock throbbing in the air, wet and sticky with pre-cum.

His hands grab my waist and he pushes me backwards until the back of my legs hit the bed.

"Sit down."

I do as he says; the silk sheets soothe my stinging arse. He lifts my feet, removing my shoes. I feel him pull my jeans off, leaving me wearing nothing but a blindfold and my socks.

I feel his hands grip the back of my head and pull it forward. His cock pushes into my mouth, hitting the back of my throat. He face-fucks me, the taste of his cock making my cock throb more.

"Kneel down in front of the bed," he whispers in a sweet, sexy voice.

I get down on my knees, my wet cock sliding against the silk sheets of the bed.

"Place your hands on the back of your head and lean down on the bed."

In my mind, I have the image of myself bent over the bed with my hands on the back of my head, my arse wide open to him.

I feel his tongue against my hole, licking, stretching it open as he pushes his tongue into me. After a few minutes, his tongue has gone, then I feel his cock head press against my hole. He rams it deep into me. I bite down into the bed to stop myself making a noise. As he pounds my arse hard, his fingers dig into my back to help steady himself. He fucks me faster. This is what I have been waiting for all day.

He doesn't last long before he growls and pushes deep into me, his cock throbbing, shooting his cum deep inside me. He holds his cock inside until his orgasm passes, then he pulls it out, my arse gaping from his fucking. I feel his cum dribbling out of me as I stay in the same position, not sure if I should move or not.

He removes my hands from my head and undoes the blindfold.

"Did you enjoy that?" he asks, still somewhat breathless.

"That was great, I enjoyed every minute." I sit on the bed and Bradley sits next to me.

"I think we have had enough for tonight. We can have more fun tomorrow."

"I would love to, babes."

"Okay, let's get to sleep."

We both lay down on the bed. I snuggle into his chest and fall into a deep sleep.

———

I wake up alone in the bed. The music has stopped but the light is still glowing in the corner. Stretching my arms and legs, the silk sheets slide against my skin. I can hear Bradley singing in the distance. He must be in the kitchen. Getting out of bed, I put on my jockstrap and shirt. The shirt isn't long enough to cover my arse, making me wish I had worn boxers instead as I head upstairs to find Bradley.

"Morning, sleepyhead," Bradley says as I walk into the kitchen.

"Morning, babes. What time is it?"

Bradley is wearing tight-fitting black boxers and a white T-shirt.

"Ten thirty. I was just finishing breakfast, then I would have woken you."

"I could hear you singing from the basement. That woke me up."

"Sorry. I always have a sing-along in the mornings. Grab a seat. The food will be ready in a minute. I can cook a breakfast."

"No need to be sorry. It's nice to hear you happy."

I take a seat at the table. The wooden seat feels cold

against my bare arse. Bradley places a plate in front of me with a full English breakfast on it. He puts his plate down and sits opposite me at the table.

"Eat up, before it goes cold," Bradley says with a smile.

We eat the breakfast with no conversation. It's nice; just what I needed after last night. It doesn't take either of us long to clear our plates.

"Do you have anything planned for today?" Bradley asks.

"Not really. Just spending the day at home."

"Well, if you're free, you can stay here with me today, if you want."

My heart skips a beat. Did I actually hear what I thought I did? There is nothing I would want more than to spend time with him.

"Are you sure, babes?" I reply, trying to sound casual about the question.

"Yes, I have nothing planned today or tonight, so if you want to stay until tomorrow, you're more than welcome."

Wow, a day and night now. I can't believe my luck.

"I've only got the clothes from last night with me."

"That's not a problem. I'll turn up the heating and you can just stay in your jock."

My cock stiffens at the thought of being almost naked around him all day.

"Okay, sounds good."

"That's settled then," Bradley says as he gets up from his chair. He walks to the side of me and leans down to give me a kiss.

"Well, get your shirt off and make yourself comfortable in the lounge," he says.

I like the way his voice is so commanding, I get off my seat and unbutton my shirt, removing it and placing it on the back of the chair.

"Much better," Bradley says as he pulls me into him, his lips touching mine as his hands slide down my back and grab my arse. I feel him grind his cock against me.

"Take a seat in the lounge. I'll clear this stuff away."

As I turn to walk towards the kitchen door, his hand slaps against my bare arse, leaving a burning handprint on my skin. Although it hurts, it still turns me on. I'm enjoying being dominated by Bradley. I walk through the hallway into the lounge and don't stop. Once out of sight, I gently rub my arse where his hand had hit me. Settling into the sofa, it feels weird sitting around in someone else's house in only a jockstrap.

After a while, Bradley appears at the door, carrying two cups. He had made us coffee. He hands me a cup, then he settles down on the sofa beside me.

"So, did you enjoy last night?" Bradley asks in a low, gruff voice.

"Yes, babes. It certainly turned me on. You definitely know how to please a man."

"Thanks, we can have more fun later, if you want."

"I'm all yours. Do what you like to me," I say with a little laugh.

"Well, that's an offer I won't refuse."

Bradley sips his coffee and stares at me, his gorgeous eyes burning into me. I start to relax, forgetting I'm only wearing my jock.

"Play eighties selection," Bradley says in his lovely, sexy voice. Music plays around the room. I begin singing along to the songs. I can't stop myself when I hear eighties music. Bradley smiles at me and watches me sing as he relaxes back into the sofa. A few songs play, then Bradley puts his cup down and stands.

"Get on your hands and knees on the sofa," he says in a demanding voice.

I put my cup down and do as I'm told. I kneel on the sofa and place my hands on the back, my arse at the right level for Bradley.

I feel his hand rub my arse, then both his hands grab my cheeks and pull them apart. He must have knelt down as I feel his tongue circling my hole, making me wet. He pushes his tongue into me a few times. Then I hear him stand up. He pulls the cheeks of my arse apart again. This time, I feel his cock head pushing against my hole. As I push back against him, he rams his cock hard and deep into me, making me arch my back as he pounds my arse.

My cock is hard, stretching the front of my jock, leaking onto the material, making it wet. Bradley's body slaps against me with every deep thrust into me, then he holds his cock deep in me and grinds his pubic hair against me, trying to get his cock as deep inside me as he can. I'm pushing back against his thrusts, my arse tingling with pleasure as he fucks me harder. I want to shout out, but after last night I know he doesn't approve of me making noise.

He is ramming his cock into me and then pulling it

fully out before ramming it back in deeper. I'm struggling to hold back my moans as he fucks me.

"I'm going to cum," he growls noisily as he hastily fucks me, then lets out a final loud growl as I feel his cock throb inside me, shooting his cum deep into me.

He continues slowly grinding against me for a while before pulling his cock out of me. I truly enjoy being fucked by his thick cock.

"Stay there," he says, breathless from the action. I watch him leave the room. He swiftly returns, carrying wipes, which he hands to me.

"Here. Clean yourself," he says, then sits on the sofa, watching me intensely as I wipe my arse clean.

"There is a toilet next to the front door. You can flush the wipes there."

I finish cleaning up and head to the toilet. When I return, Bradley is still sitting on the sofa.

"That was good," he says as I walk back in the room.

"Sure was. You can fuck me anytime."

I sit down next to Bradley and snuggle into him as we continue listening to the music.

We must have drifted off to sleep together as I wake up several hours later, still laying on Bradley. As I stir, so does he.

"What time is it?" Bradley asks.

"I'm not sure. My watch is downstairs."

Bradley gets up from the sofa and wanders out of the room, then soon returns. "It's just past noon. Would you like another drink?"

"Yes, please, babes. Would you like a hand?"

"No, I'm okay, thanks. You stay there and rest. You will need your energy for later," he says with a smile.

Bradley comes back with more drinks and sits down next to me again. "Shall we watch a movie?" he asks.

"If you want. I'm pleased being here with you."

"Show theatre," he says in his deep voice. To my amazement, a panel in the corner of the room slides open as a huge fifty-inch screen glides out automatically into the room.

"What type of film would you enjoy?"

"Let's have an action film, babes."

Bradley calls into the room again and the film he names plays on the screen. The sound fills the room. We spend several hours watching two films, snuggled up together on the sofa.

$\mathcal{W}$hen the second movie finishes, Bradley commands the screen to close and it glides back into the wall. That answers where the TV was.

"Would you like something to eat, maybe a takeaway? Which do you prefer? Chinese or Indian?"

"Indian is my favourite."

"Okay, I will order various dishes for us to share."

"My wallet is downstairs in my trousers."

"Don't worry about that. It's my treat."

"Okay, if you're sure."

Bradley gets up and goes to order the takeaway. It still feels weird sitting around in someone else's house in just a jockstrap, but I also like the fact he doesn't mind seeing me almost naked.

Bradley comes back in the room. "It should be about thirty minutes; do you want to come in the kitchen? We can eat at the table?"

"Yeah, sure." I get up and follow him into the

kitchen and stand, watching him as he lays out the table. Opening the fridge, he pulls out another bottle of pink Prosecco.

"A little drink while we wait?"

"I won't say no, babes."

Bradley pours two glasses and places the bottle on the table, then hands me a glass. As I take it, he leans in and kisses me. His other hand grabs my cock and lightly massages it inside my jock as his tongue entwines with mine.

"I will enjoy fucking you later," he says in between kisses.

My cock stiffens in his hand. He slides his hand around behind me and grabs my arse, pulling me against him. Grinding his hard cock against mine, he continues exploring my mouth with his tongue. Time must have flown by as the doorbell rings.

"Supper has arrived," he says as he puts his glass down on the side. Picking up his wallet, he goes to the front door. He does not seem to care that his cock is hard and obvious as it tents his boxers, leaving me standing in the kitchen with my rock-hard cock stretching my jock. By the time he comes back, his cock has gone soft again, and he unloads the bag of Indian food onto the table.

"Grab a seat."

I sit at the table; he had ordered various dishes and there must be enough food for at least four people.

"Help yourself. Don't be shy."

"Thanks, this looks lovely."

"You're welcome; now eat up." He refills my glass as I fill my plate from the takeaway cartons.

We eat the meal in relative silence, both enjoying the food and drink.

"Oh, babes, I'm full. Sorry, I can't eat anymore."

"That's okay. I've had enough as well."

"What are you going to do with what's left?"

"I will put it in the fridge. My cleaner often has my leftover takeaways; I always seem to order too much."

"At least it won't go to waste."

I watch Bradley as he puts the leftover food into the fridge and then clears the plates and cutlery into the dishwasher. Once the table is clear, he walks back over and takes my hand.

"Come with me," he says, pulling me up from the chair and leading me out of the kitchen towards the door to the sex room.

He stops at the door again. "Are you ready for more?"

"Yes, babes. Do what you like."

Opening the door, he heads down the stairs and I follow him. This time, he walks to the corner of the room where the sex swing is standing. My cock stirs in my jock as I realise he is going to fuck me on the swing; it's what I have been waiting for since I arrived.

"Leave your jock on and get up into the swing," he says in a deep, soothing voice.

I clamber into the swing, laying on my back. I can see myself in the mirrors above me. Bradley walks to the side of the swing and grabs my left arm, pulling it up against the chains that support the cradle. He tightens a leather strap around my wrist, securing it to the chain. Walking to the other side, he does the same to my right arm.

"I'm going to pleasure you until you beg me to stop," he whispers, then walks back to where my legs are hanging off the swing.

He grabs my right leg and pulls it up to the chain, shifting me in the swing so my arse is easily accessible, then he straps my leg to the chain. He does the same with my left leg. Now I cannot move, strapped to the swing with my legs wide open, my arse completely exposed to him.

I watch him closely as he slides a mirror panel on the wall open. Inside are neatly organised sex toys: various dildos, butt plugs, leather straps, and whips. On shelves are bottles of lubricant and other leather items of clothing.

Bradley picks up a pair of leather gloves and slips them onto his hands, holding them against his face. He breathes intensely and I hear him release a quiet moan of pleasure.

He removes his T-shirt and boxers, his cock already semi-hard. Reaching to another shelf, he picks up a metal cock ring and slides it over his cock, which stiffens even more, enhanced by the ring.

"Are you ready to play?" Bradley asks in a commanding voice.

"Yes, babes."

"Don't call me babes in this room. You must call me sir," he shouts furiously at me.

"Sorry, sir," I reply in a low whimper of a voice.

Realising he wants to be dominant in his sex room, I'm content to play the submissive.

"Do not speak unless I give you permission," he says in a low growling voice.

He takes a bottle of lubricant off the shelf and pumps it into his gloved hand. Moving back to my arse, I feel his cold, gloved hand rub lubricant against me. His gloved finger gradually pushes into my hole. I have to hold back my moans of pleasure as his finger slides in and out of me, circling inside me, stretching my sphincter muscles. Next, I feel two fingers push deep into me as he twists them and pulls them out.

The force of his fingers fucking me make me swing back and forth. Looking in the mirror above me, I can see his fingers sliding in and out my arse. His cock is now harder than I have ever seen it before as he continues finger-fucking me. The muscles in my arse are now loose as they relax into the rhythm.

Bradley pulls his fingers out of me and goes back over to where the sex toys are. Picking up a dildo the size of his own cock, he rubs lubricant all over it, then returns to my arse.

I have to bite my lip as he pushes its full length into me, the girth stretching my hole open. With no hesitation, he fucks me with the dildo, pulling it almost fully out before ramming it back into me. I'm trying my best to stifle the noises of pleasure. After several minutes, he pulls the dildo out and drops it to the floor. I watch him in the mirrors as he moves between my legs and rams his own cock deep into me. Grabbing the chains, he pulls me towards him each time he fucks me.

My cock is throbbing hard and leaking pre-cum as he continues fucking me. The head of my cock has escaped from the jock. I want to grab it, but my hands are strapped to the chains. His breathing quickens and he growls as he fucks me faster. I know he is about to cum.

Several quicker fucks and he rams himself deep into me. I feel his cock throbbing, his warm cum shooting deep inside as he roars out like a wild bear.

I'm as breathless as he is, my arse fucked hard. He pulls his cock out of me and grabs another somewhat larger dildo from the rack and covers it in lube. He moves back to my arse and shoves it deep into me, stretching me a little more. I cannot help letting out a whimper as he holds it deep in me. His other gloved hand grips tightly around my cock and slides my foreskin back and forth over the head.

It doesn't take long before I shoot cum up to my face, my arse gripping tight against the dildo. I'm overcome with pleasurable feelings deep inside me.

"That's it. Let it go," Bradley growls at me.

The biggest load of cum I have ever shot lands against me as my body spasms with pleasure.

Letting go of my cock, he continues to slide the dildo in and out of me until my arse can't take anymore.

"Stop, please stop," I plead.

Bradley pulls the dildo out of me. My arse is gaping and throbbing deep within. Now I have been well and truly fucked.

"Have you had enough?"

"Yes, sir."

Bradley's cock has now softened, so he pulls off the cock ring and removes the gloves, dropping them both on the floor. He unstraps my arms and legs and helps me out of the swing. My legs feel like jelly from both being strapped up and the hard fuck I had received.

He pulls me into his arms and kisses me fervently.

"Do you want to sleep?," he asks.

"Yes, please."

We both walk over to the bed and climb onto it. I cuddle into Bradley, my arse numb from all the action. He wraps his arms around me, my head laying on his chest, I drift off into a deep sleep.

7

J must have been very tired as I wake up in bed alone, the now-familiar light glowing in the corner of the room. My arse still feels raw from last night. The cool silk sheets are wrapped around my belly and legs. I stretch, feeling very satisfied. Bradley undoubtedly knows how to please me. I lay there, unsure of the time, then I hear Bradley walking down the stairs. He appears in the room, the low light shining on one side of his gorgeous, naked body, highlighting the well-toned muscles and hairy chest.

"Morning, I was not expecting you to be awake," he says as he walks towards the bed.

"Morning, babes. What time is it?"

"It's only 6:30." He climbs onto the bed and straddles me. As he lowers himself to kiss me, I feel his hard cock press against me through the silk sheets.

His soft, wet lips meet mine as his chest hair brushes over my nipples. He is a different man to the one who strapped me into the swing last night; gentle and loving, giving soft kisses as he wriggles around on top of me, shifting the covers off my body.

He slides his legs in between mine and uses his knees to push my legs apart, making me lift them up and wrap them around his body. Shifting up my body, I feel his hard cock hit my hole.

Grabbing my arms, he pushes them back over my head and holds them to the bed as he lifts his body, arching his back. My arse is wet from the night's action and sweat as his cock pushes into me with ease. I moan with pleasure.

Slowly, he thrusts deeper into me as my legs tighten around his body.

Moving to hold both my arms with one hand, his other plays with my nipple bar as his cock thrusts in and out of me. His breathing quickens and the low moans get louder, becoming deep grunts with each push into me. I know he is near the edge. He shifts position. Grabbing my thighs, he pulls me back against him as he rams his cock into me.

Roaring noisily, two more deep pushes, and then his cock throbs deep inside, shooting his cum.

He pulls his cock out of me and falls on top of me, panting for breath. I close my arms around him, lightly stroking his hairy back. After a while, he shifts on the bed, turning me on my side without a word and snuggles up against me, his soft, wet cock squashed against me as his arms pull me into his chest.

We both drift off to sleep again.

A few hours must have passed when we both wake up, still in each other's arms.

"Morning again," he says, smiling at me.

"Morning. I have had a wonderful weekend."

"Glad to hear. I will make breakfast. Why don't you have a shower, then come upstairs."

"Will do, babes."

Bradley gives me a gentle kiss, then slides off the bed. I watch him walk to the stairs, his arse looking amazing in the low light of the room, the only part of his body not tanned. He must wear Speedos when tanning.

Once he has disappeared up the stairs, I get up and have a shower, making sure I clean myself well. It's the first shower I have had since Friday night. Then, I get dressed and head up to the kitchen. Bradley must have showered as he is now wearing blue chino-style shorts and a pink shirt, looking as gorgeous as ever.

"Hey, grab a seat. You timed that right. Breakfast is just ready."

"Thanks, babes."

He puts a cooked breakfast down in front of me and another for himself. "Enjoy."

We both eat in silence until our plates are empty of food.

"Regrettably, I have to head out early this morning. I have a few meetings today. I hope you don't mind."

"No problem. I have had a great weekend, anyway."

"My pleasure. I have enjoyed it as well."

After breakfast, I say my goodbyes to Bradley and

head home. I have definitely had a good fuck this weekend so I'm heading home nice and satisfied. With any luck, I will hear from him again. He doesn't seem boyfriend material but he certainly knows how to fuck.

Maybe we will get together again soon?

8

***

Six months later

Since we met six months ago, I have spent several nights and weekends with Bradley. He is a lovely, caring man and can be extremely dominating in the bedroom, which is totally my kind of guy. Gradually, during the time we have spent together, he has revealed more about himself. I now know he is a high-flying businessman at the head of a huge company. When you first meet him outside of his home environment, you would have no idea how successful and wealthy he really is, not that I'm chasing his money. He is a wonderful guy who gives me what I want sexually and I'm sure I kind of give him an escape from his business world.

When we first met, he said he wasn't interested in a relationship, just no strings sex. But I'm starting to get the feeling he is growing to the idea of something a bit more serious. He has started sending flowers to my

59

home and last weekend he gave me an expensive watch as a present. I would be very happy to be in a full-on relationship with him. But I won't push things with him as I enjoy the time we get to spend together.

As for me, I'm a happy-go-lucky, chubby guy who still can't believe that this hot guy wants to spend time with me.

I'm having my lunch in the staff room with the girls from work when my phone begins to vibrate in my pocket. As I pull it out, Bradley's face is smiling at me from the screen.

'Hello, handsome,' I say. My face flushes and my hands become clammy whenever I hear from him. The girls give me a sly look as they know it is Bradley on the phone.

'Morning, gorgeous, how's your day going?'

'Same old routine, babes, people moaning at me on the phones. How are you?'

'I'm well, thanks, I've not long escaped from a meeting, I have another one in a few minutes. The reason for my call, I've been invited to an awards dinner next weekend, and I wondered if you would like to accompany me. I will have to work a little whilst there, but we would get plenty of time together. Would you be able to get Friday and Monday off work?'

Wow, my heart is beating fast now. This is a big step, introducing me to his work colleagues. I have to keep control of my voice as, emotionally, I'm shocked and excited.

'I should be able to, when do you need to know?'

'Can you let me know by 3pm? So, I can get the flights booked.'

'Flights?' My voice became noticeably high pitched. The girls all stare at me intently, wanting to know what's being said.

'Yes, the awards are in New York, is that ok?'

I cover the phone with my hand. 'Holy crap, he wants to take me to New York with him.' Now my hands are shaking with excitement. The girls start gossiping as I get back to the phone.

'Yeah, no problem, babes, I will check with my manager now and let you know.'

'Okay, that's great. Can you drop me a message? I will be in meetings all afternoon.'

'Will do,' I reply. I'm sure he can hear the excitement in my voice.

'I must dash, catch up later.'

'Okay, message you soon.'

Bradley hangs up the phone and I let out a scream.

'Oh my God, he wants to take me to New York for an awards dinner.'

'You can't miss out on that, sounds like he is getting serious,' Mandy says.

'I know, sorry, girls, I must find Harry and check I can get the time off.' I jump up from my seat, forgetting about my lunch as I run out of the staff room, screaming to myself.

I find Harry sitting in his office and explain to him about the New York trip and he agrees that I can have the days off. I'm so excited about the weekend. I run back to the staff room. Jumping and clapping as I go through the door.

'Harry said yes, I'm going to New York, girls,' I scream out to them. Mandy runs over and gives me a huge hug. 'I'm so pleased for you, this is all going so well for you,' she says.

'Thanks, I can't believe it, I'm all nervous now about meeting his work colleagues.'

'Don't you start worrying about that, he has invited you, so he must want you to meet them, enjoy the trip,' Mandy says with her mothering tone. She does take care of me.

'You're right, I'm so excited.'

I send a message to Bradley to tell him I can make the trip. I spend the rest of the afternoon waiting for a reply. After work, I head home to decide on what I should take to New York with me. I know it is not until next weekend, but packing takes a lot of planning.

About 6pm I receive a reply from Bradley.

Excellent, I will call you later to get your passport details and discuss the trip. Looking forward to it.

I was on a high for the rest of the days before the trip, looking forward to spending time with Bradley. We are flying at 12:05pm, so I have to make my way over to his house on Friday morning. He had arranged for a car to take us to the airport.

When I get to his house, I ring the doorbell and wait for him to open the door.

'Hey, gorgeous, are you ready for the trip?' he says, gesturing me into the house.

'I can't wait, I've never been to New York,' I say as I drag my case into the house.

Bradley closes the door then pulls me into his arms, his lips meet mine and his tongue slides into my mouth. I hug him tight as his tongue tussles with mine; we kiss passionately. After a while, he breaks away from me.

'I've been waiting all morning to do that,' Bradley says.

Bradley is certainly showing more affection than the early days. I want to tell him how much I have missed him since we last met, but hold back. I don't want to turn him off me.

'The car should be here in about fifteen minutes, have you remembered your passport?'

'Of course.'

'Good, we are all set to go.'

He pulls me back into his arms. This time his hard cock pushes against my leg.

'Someone is happy to see me, for sure,' I say with a smile.

'Yes, and looking forward to lots of fun this weekend.'

Bradley kisses me deeply as he slides his right hand down the back of my jeans, his fingers sliding between my arse cheeks and pressing against my hole. My cock stiffens in my pants; I could drop my jeans and let him fuck me against the wall in his entrance hall, but I resist the urge.

'So, where are we staying in New York?' I ask, trying to distract myself from wanting him to fuck me. Bradley removes his hand from my jeans and holds onto my waist, hugging me close to him so I could still feel his hard cock.

'The same hotel where the awards dinner is being held, I'm not telling you the name as I want to see your face when you see it.'

'You could at least tell me the name of the hotel, I probably won't have heard of it.'

'No, the weekend I have planned is all a surprise.'

'Okay, I will wait.' I know from experience it is not worth trying to get information from Bradley unless he wants to tell you. The doorbell rings, making as both jump as we had relaxed in each other's arms.

'Here we go,' Bradley says. We pick up our cases and Bradley opens the door.

I was expecting a taxi driver to be waiting, instead a chauffeur is standing on the doorstep.

'May I take your bags, sir?' he asks.

Bradley passes his case to him and he holds out his other hand for mine. Taking the cases, he walks down the path and I see the black executive car parked on the road.

'Flashy car,' I say to Bradley as he locks the door behind us.

'All paid for by the company, as is the weekend, so relax and enjoy yourself. Don't worry about the cost of things.'

He has learned that about me, money matters, my job in the contact centre only pays a low wage so I have to think about the cost of the things I do.

'Okay, babes, I will try.'

Bradley gives me a little smile and gets into the car

as the chauffeur holds the door open for us. The inside of the car has white leather seats, the kind you sink into and snuggle as they are so comfortable. Bradley leans over and gives me a gentle kiss on the lips. I'm a little taken back, as he doesn't normally show affection in public.

'I hope you enjoy this trip,' he says.

'I always enjoy spending time with you.'

He reaches over and holds my hand, his warm, strong fingers entwine with mine as his grip tightens, giving me a warm feeling of security inside.

'I'm enjoying getting to know you too.'

We spend the entire journey to the airport holding hands in the car. Pulling up at the airport the chauffeur opens the door so we can get out and hands us our cases. I see Bradley palming him a ten pound note as they shake hands.

We trundle our cases into the airport and head for the check in desks.

'Wow, look at the queue,' I say as I notice the amount of people waiting to check their luggage.

'Don't worry, we're not joining that queue,' Bradley says as he heads towards the business class check-in desk. I should have guessed he would be travelling business class. Once we had dealt with the cases, I follow Bradley to the priority departure lane. I feel like a celebrity as we speed through the security checks into the departure lounge.

'Where shall we sit?' I ask

'In the first class lounge, I think.'

'Really?'

'Yes, as I said this is all on the company, so enjoy being spoiled.'

'Okay, I will pretend I'm a celebrity,' I say with a little laugh.

'You're my celebrity,' he says, giving me another smile.

'Ah, babes, that's lovely.'

'Come on, follow me,' he says, heading off in the direction of the lounges.

The ladies on the reception desk to the lounge are lovely, I find it funny being called 'sir', but I'm enjoying this special treatment. Me and Bradley do live in different worlds; I normally fly with budget airlines and scramble for seats in the departure lounge.

We find seats in the first class lounge; the place is huge with comfy sofas and chairs spread around. There is an array of various self-serve food on offer and an open bar where you can have any drink you like. There's also a separate dining area with a hot food menu. I catch Bradley staring at me out the corner of my eye.

'Why are you staring at me?'

'I'm enjoying the wonderful look on your face; you're so surprised and appreciative of all this.'

'I've never been in a lounge like this, how the other half live.'

'Well, you're living it now.'

'True, and it's a lovely experience, really nice of you to invite me.'

'Don't be silly, I wanted you to come with me and to share this weekend with you.'

As one of the staff walk by, Bradley asks politely for

two glasses of Champagne, which they go off to fetch, returning and placing them on the table for us.

'Here's to a wonderful weekend,' Bradley says as he raises his glass. I pick mine up and our glasses clink together. 'Cheers.'

We go and help ourselves to some food and bring it back to our seats, spending about forty minutes in the lounge before our gate displays boarding. Then we head down to the gate. Boarding the plane, we are called forward first and walk down the jetway to the plane. The stewardess welcomes us on board and we take our seats in row one. This is my first time in business class, it seems strange having all this space. I watch people as they walk past us. Once everyone has boarded, the plane doors are locked and we listen to the emergency procedures before the flight attendants take their seats for take-off.

'Are you okay?' Bradley asks.

'Yeah, I'm enjoying the experience.'

'Good,' Bradley replies before leaning over and giving me a lingering kiss on the lips. I must have blushed slightly.

'Sorry. have I embarrassed you?'

'No, it's just this is the first time you have kissed me like that in public.'

'Well it won't be the last,' he replies with a smile.

He holds my hand as the engines roar and the plane lunges forward along the runway. I grip his hand tight as the plane lifts into the air. Once we are in the air, the seat belt signs go out and the stewardess comes over to us.

'Good afternoon, sir, can I get you a drink?' she asks Bradley.

'Can I have Champagne, please?'

'Certainly, sir, and for yourself?' she asks me.

'I will have Champagne as well, please.'

She hands us menu cards and heads off to get the drinks.

'This is such a wonderful experience,' I say to Bradley.

'I'm glad you are enjoying yourself,' he says, giving me another kiss. I didn't realise Bradley was so comfortable with public displays of affection, but I'm loving every moment.

The stewardess returns with our Champagne and takes our food orders from the menu. We chat away about what we have done during the week. After about fifteen minutes, she returns with our food and refills our glasses. The rest of the flight we spend chatting and drinking. The Champagne is starting to go to my head by the time we land.

*a*s we exit into the arrivals area we are met by a
driver holding up a sign with Bradley's name
on it. He introduces himself and takes our cases as we
follow him out to the car, another big executive vehicle.
The car drives us to the hotel in the city, pulling up
outside the Grand Tower hotel. The driver opens the
door for us to get out of the car, whilst the hotel porter
collects the cases from the trunk.

The hotel has marble-clad walls at the entrance. As
we walked into the lobby, it was a huge, open space with
bright white and black walls. White and shiny, grey
leather sofas are arranged by a fire encased in glass. The
reception desk along one wall is white with a black top
and a huge picture along the wall behind it of several
men's faces wearing sunglasses. A single vase of yellow
tulips sits at one end of the desk.

Bradley walks to the desk and introduces himself.
The lady is extremely polite and gives the porter a key.

'The penthouse suite,' she says to the porter, then

turns back to Bradley. 'Please do not hesitate to ask for anything you require, sir.' She continues smiling at Bradley.

'Thank you,' Bradley replies and begins to follow the porter towards the lift. I walk along beside him, still taking in the surroundings. This is definitely a five-star hotel. We ride the lift to the top floor, there are only two doors on this floor, the porter opens the door for us and we walk into the suite.

As my eyes survey the room, the porter asks Bradley if he wants him to explain where everything is in the room. Bradley politely declines and gives him a tip. He closes the door behind him as he leaves us alone in the suite.

'What do you think?' Bradley asks.

'It's amazing, this place is bigger than my flat.'

'Have a wander around; it's all ours for a few days.'

The living room has a blue, white and grey carpet with a block pattern design and a large, white leather sofa and two high-backed, blue leather chairs. There is a huge TV screen on the wall and a desk to one side and a white, six-seater dining table with leather chairs to the other. All the furniture is arranged to give the best views out of the floor-to-ceiling windows, with a skyline view over the city.

'It's so lovely,' I say as I walk towards the door to the bedroom. Bradley watches me, his own enjoyment coming from my surprised looks.

The bedroom has a huge, white, king size bed with a padded leather headboard along the wall with pictures hanging above that. There are more huge windows with amazing views over the city. Another door leads into the bathroom, which has floor-to-ceiling white marble, and a huge, oblong jacuzzi bath with two rainfall shower-heads suspended above it.

'Do you like the place?' Bradley asks.

'Like it? I love it. If Mandy could see me now, she would be gobsmacked.'

Bradley pulls me into his arms, hugging me tight as his lips brush against mine.

'Well, now we're finally alone, we can have some fun,' he says as his cock stiffens against my leg.

I kiss him back, pulling him tighter against me. 'Where would you like me, sir?'

'Come with me.' Bradley takes my hand and leads me back into the living room, walking me over to one of the blue leather chairs. Standing me in front of the chair, his hands caress my face as he kisses me, his tongue exploring deep into my mouth. He pulls away from me and slowly unbuttons my shirt, admiring my smooth, hairless body, as my chest and belly are revealed to him. I hear a moan of approval.

'I see you did as I asked,' he says in a soft whisper.

'Yes, is this smooth enough for you?' I ask.

Sliding his hands around my waist, he kisses and nibbles at my neck. My cock stiffens in my pants as his hands slide to my belly. His right hand gliding up to my nipple, he squeezes it hard, making me wince in pain. I feel his mouth move down from my neck as he drags his wet tongue along my skin, until he reaches my nipple, softly circling it with his tongue.

He removes my shirt from my shoulders and it drops

to the floor. Bradley lowers himself to the floor, kissing my chest and belly on his way down. Undoing my belt and jeans, he pulls them to the floor. His face presses against my stiff cock in my white briefs and he kisses my cock through the material.

'Shall I see if your cock is smooth as well?'

'Yes, sir,' I reply. My breath quickens as my cock throbs in my pants.

Bradley slides my pants to the floor, releasing my hard cock.

'Very nice,' he says as he sees my hairless cock and balls.

His tongue circles the head of my cock, pushing my foreskin back off the head as I moan with pleasure.

'Sit down,' he says in a commanding voice.

I sit on the chair and he remains kneeling. He removes my shoes and lifts my feet free of my clothes, tossing them to one side.

I'm now sitting naked in the chair as he stands.

'You're gorgeous without body hair.'

'Thank you, sir,' I reply, knowing he likes me to call him sir.

I stare at Bradley as he undoes his own shirt, his dark-toned, hairy body looks as mouth-watering as ever. Dropping his shirt to the floor, he undoes his trousers and pushes them along with his pants to the floor. His hard, throbbing, eight-inch cock points at me. He slips off his shoes and steps out of his clothes. Now standing naked, he wiggles side-to-side, making his cock wave around in front of me. I want to get off the chair and take his cock in my mouth, but I don't move, waiting to see what he does next.

'Lift your hands off the arms of the chair,' he commands.

I do as I'm told. I watch Bradley climb onto the arms of the chair, kneeling, straddling across me so his hard cock is now inches from my face.

'Lick my cock.'

I slide my tongue over the head of his cock and he moans with pleasure. After a minute, his hands grab the sides of my head and pushes a couple of inches of his cock into my mouth. I suck his cock as he begins to slowly thrust it into my mouth, getting deeper with each push forward. I place my hands on his thighs, trying to control how deep his cock gets into my mouth. Bradley grabs my hands and pushes them behind my head holding them tightly to the back of the chair. His thrusting gets faster as he tries to force his full length into my throat.

My cock is throbbing, pre-cum leaking and running down the shaft, as he face-fucks me harder. My hands held tight behind my head, I'm unable to stop him ramming his cock deep into my throat. His pace quickens as his breathing becomes erratic I know he is about to cum. Two more deep thrust before his thick warm cum explodes into my mouth. As he roars out loud, I try to swallow his load. Once I have sucked his cock dry, he pulls it from my mouth and climbs down off the chair. Kneeling, he lowers his mouth over my pre-cum-soaked cock. Taking it fully into his mouth he sucks and licks the head. Within minutes I'm pushing up into his mouth and moan loudly as my load shoots into his throat. My hairless body sweats and sticks to the leather of the chair. Bradley licks my cock clean before standing. He pulls me up out of the chair and hugs me tight to his hairy body, rubbing himself against my skin. Kissing me deeply, I can taste my cum in his mouth.

'That was great,' Bradley says.

'Sure was, babes. Every time with you is great.'

'Let's have a quick shower and get some sleep before we head out to dinner later,' he says.

'Okay.'

We share the shower. The huge rain showerheads pour water down on us as we lather each other's bodies. My hands linger on Bradley's lovely, hairy chest. Once we had showered, we dry ourselves, then climb into the huge bed. Bradley snuggles up behind me. Having removed my own hair from my body as Bradley had asked me to do, I could feel his hair against my back, which sent tingling feelings down my spine. His pubic hair and soft cock snuggle against my arse. We both drift off into a contented sleep.

10

*W*aking an hour later, Bradley is already up. I lay looking out the huge windows across the New York skyline; the lights from the buildings seem to be twinkling against the star-filled sky. I still cannot believe how lucky I am to be here with Bradley. After a while Bradley comes walking back into the bedroom. He is still naked, so I smile at him and admire his lovely body.

'Evening, gorgeous,' he says as he sits on the bed next to me, running his hand along the side on my smooth body.

'Good evening, handsome.'

'I love your body smooth, it suits you.'

'All for you, babes.' Bradley leans down and gives me a kiss.

'We best unpack and get dressed for dinner,' he says, getting up from the bed.

'Okay,' I reply as I get up from the bed.

We both remain naked as we unpack our cases and I

cannot resist sneaking looks at Bradley. I hang up my clothes in the wardrobe.

'Where are we eating this evening?'

'In the hotel restaurant, we have to dine with two of my work colleagues and their partners. I hope you don't mind.'

'No, of course not, this is your business trip after all.'

'Good, I'm sure you will like them. They will definitely like you.'

'I hope so.' A wave of nervousness flows through me at the thought of meeting these people.

'What shall I wear for dinner?'

'Shirt and trousers will be fine.'

We both get dressed. There are a selection of after-shaves on the dressing table. Bradley picks one up and sprays it onto me, before selecting another one for himself.

'You look and smell wonderful,' he says.

'So do you.'

Bradley pulls me into his arms and gives me a long, lingering kiss.

'Are you nervous?'

'Yes, a little. I always get nervous when I first meet people and I don't want to let you down.'

'You won't let me down. Just be yourself, relax and enjoy the evening.'

'I will try.' He gives me another kiss and a hug.

'Okay, let's hit the restaurant and remember it's all paid for, so eat and drink anything you want.'

'Okay.'

We leave the suite and get the lift to the restaurant,

which is on the floor below us, so it also has skyline views of the city. As we reach the restaurant door, my hands begin to sweat, the nerves of meeting his colleagues building inside.

'Good evening, sir,' the restaurant host says.

'We are meeting friends for dinner a table in the name of Franklin,' Bradley says.

'Oh, yes, sir, the other guests are already here. Please follow me.'

I follow behind Bradley as we walk towards the back of the restaurant where I see a large, round table with two couples chatting away with each other. They all stand as we get to the table the men shaking Bradley's hand, then he gives the ladies a kiss on the cheek.

'Evening, everyone,' Bradley says 'This is David.' The first man, tall and slim with blonde hair, holds out his hand to me.

'Good evening, David, I'm Robert and this is my wife, Michelle.' I shake his hand and Michelle kisses my cheek.

The second man, shorter and a little chubby with a bald head, holds his hand out. 'Evening, I'm Daniel and this is Susan.'

I shake his hand. 'Evening.' Then I give Susan a kiss.

'Lovely to meet you,' She says.

'You too,' I say.

'I see the drink is already flowing,' Bradley says, drawing attention away from me.

'It is, indeed, old chap,' Robert says.

We all sit down at the table and Robert pours out two glasses of Champagne for Bradley and me.

The conversation is about work and the current performance of different areas of the company. Whilst they chat away, I work out that Robert is the head of US marketing and Daniel is the head of service delivery worldwide. No one has mentioned where Bradley comes into things. We have never really discussed his work in depth. I know he is in charge of a large company, but I have no idea what they sell. I start to zone out of the conversation and look around the restaurant. It seems the whole place is filled with business people dining with their wives and partners by their side.

Suddenly, I'm drawn back into the conversation as Robert mentions the awards dinner.

'So, tomorrow after the morning meeting we return to the hotel in plenty of time for the awards.'

'I'm sure you will walk away with an award tomorrow, Bradley,' Daniel says.

'Let's not jump to conclusions, I'm up against some very big business names,' Bradley says.

'You are, but turnover in the company has trebled this year and our takeover of several growing social media companies means we are at the top of the game,' Robert says.

A waiter arrives at the table.

'Good evening,' he says as he hands us menus. 'Would you like any more drinks?' he asks.

'Yes, two more bottles of Champagne, please,' Bradley says.

'Certainly, sir,' he says as he walks away from the table.

I look at the menu and take in a gasp of breath at

the prices. Bradley told me not to worry about the prices but one meal here would pay for my month's food.

'What do you fancy?' Bradley asks me, giving me a cheeky smile.

'I like the sound of the grilled swordfish,' I reply, smiling back at him.

'That does sound nice, I think I will have the same.'

The waiter returns with the Champagne, placing the two bottles in ice buckets on the table and removing the old one.

'Are you ready to order?' he asks politely.

'We are, ladies first,' Bradley says.

Everyone orders their meals and the waiter leaves the table.

'I think we should end the work talk now, the ladies must be bored. We can finalise things tomorrow at the meeting,' Bradley says.

This gives us all the opportunity to chat about our flights and the hotel, general chitchat. I note that nobody asks me any questions about who I am. I will ask Bradley about that later and also what he actually does for this company.

The food arrives, and it is delicious. The conversation slows whilst we eat our food. I can sense I am becoming giggly from all the Champagne. Once we had eaten all three courses and had coffee, Bradley suggests we call it a night, as the meeting is early in the morning.

We say goodnight to them all and head back to our suite.

'So, was it as bad as you thought?' Bradley asks as we get out of the lift.

'I was nervous, but it was a nice evening. They seem like nice people.'

'They are. Both Robert and Daniel have been with the company for over five years now.'

Bradley opens the door to the suite and we head inside.

'I keep meaning to ask you, what do you do in this company?' I ask.

'I own the company, we are a holding company taking over other established companies that are beginning to become successful, those that seem like they will grow in the future.'

'You own the company,' I repeat with surprise in my voice.

'Yes, I never told you when we met, as many guys chase me because of the money and power, but you seemed different. Only interested in me as a person, which I liked.'

'I don't know what to say. You must be mega wealthy, you could have any man you want.'

'I could, that's true, but I chose you.'

My face flushes at his words. 'But what do you see in me? I don't have much, just a little flat in town?'

'It's not about what you do or don't have, it's about you as a person, you make me smile and sex with you is great.'

Bradley walks over to me and holds me tight to him. 'You're gorgeous, sweet and untainted by money and power and I like that,' he says, then gives me a kiss.

'Well, I'm happy to stay around as long as you want me to.'

'Good, well, we have both had a lot of Champagne tonight, let's get some sleep,' he says, kissing me again.

We both go to the bedroom strip naked and snuggle together. In bed, his hairy body presses against me from behind and his arms hold me tight. I feel secure and comforted as we fall into a deep sleep.

11

I'm woken by Bradley moving around behind me, I feel his hard, wet cock rubbing against me.

'Morning, handsome,' I say as I snuggle back against him.

'Morning, gorgeous,' he says, softly kissing the back of my neck.

His hand slides around my waist and pulls me closer to him as his cock parts my arse cheeks. I push back against him as he pushes into me, his cock sliding into my hot, sweaty arse with ease. He begins to slowly thrust into me; his breath is heavy against my ear as his hand moves up my belly and reaches my nipple.

He squeezes and twists my nipple, sending pleasurable feelings through my chest as I moan out loud. His breath begins to quicken as his thrusts become faster. My cock now hard and leaking, as he pushes his full length deep into me. Our legs entwine as he slams himself deeper into me. A few harder thrusts as he pushes his cock deep inside me, growling like a bear into my ears. His cock throbs deep within me as it shoots its load.

Bradley holds me tight, his cock still in me as his breathing gradually returns to normal.

'That was a great way to wake up,' I say as I turn to face him, his cock pulling out of me.

'It was, indeed,' he says as he kisses me deeply.

He wraps his legs around mine and continues kissing me passionately.

'I have to get up, shower and get ready for my meeting.'

'Okay.'

'What are you going to do this morning? We should be back from the meeting about 1pm.'

'I will get some breakfast, then probably have a look around the hotel. I noticed there are some shops on the ground floor. I might even venture outside to the shops nearby.'

'That sounds nice, do you have some money for shopping?' he asks.

'Yes, I have money with me.'

'Okay, if you need any extra, let me know.'

'I will be fine.' Remembering what he said last night about guys chasing his money.

'Good,' he says, giving me another kiss before he climbs off the bed. I watch his arse closely as he walks towards the bathroom, it's very tight with few hairs and dimples in his cheeks. I hear the shower switch on as I lay looking up at the ceiling. Thinking about what Bradley had said the night before, the fact that he owns the company. I had no idea, not that it changes the way I think about him. The more time I spend with him, the closer I'm getting to him. He may be a high-flying businessman with lots of money but I'm getting to know the real Bradley, the man behind the corporate mask.

The shower switches off and after a few minutes Bradley walks back into the bedroom. His white towel wrapped around his waist emphasizes his deep tanned body. He looks like a model with his dark brown, wet hair dripping onto his face. The hair on his chest is damp and curls into the centre of his chest.

'What are you thinking about?' he asks.

'How wonderfully handsome you are and how lucky I am to have you in my life.'

Bradley smiles, his teeth white as snow. 'I'm the lucky one,' he says. Removing his towel, he dries off his legs and drops the towel on the floor. His soft cock looks nice and tasty as it flops around when he walks across the room to the wardrobe.

I continue watching him as he gets dressed, he looks stunningly handsome wearing his business suit. I can't resist him, so I clamber out of bed and give him a hug and kiss.

'You're so handsome,' I say and he kisses me back.

'Thanks, you have a wonderful morning,' he says. His hands hold the sides of my face and his tongue explores my mouth. My cock begins to stiffen again. He grips my cock tight. 'Make sure you leave this alone; I will deal with it later.' He is such a lovely guy and I do like the way he takes control and tells me what to do. He has just the right amount of each character to keep me happy. He gives me one last kiss before he heads out.

I get showered and dressed, then head to the restaurant for breakfast. I could have ordered room service but I want to experience the whole hotel. The breakfast is fantastic; there isn't a self-serve buffet like I normally get at the hotels I've stayed in before. It was a complete waiter service with a huge choice of items on the menu, including Buck's Fizz, so I couldn't resist spoiling myself. I have a full English breakfast with toast, then fruit with yoghurt, all washed down with two glasses of Buck's Fizz. Once I had eaten, I go down to the hotel shops for a browse. They are all little boutique shops with prices to match the hotel; one T-shirt that caught my eye was $300. As lovely as it is, I'm not spending that much on clothes, so I head out into the street.

The street is full of people rushing around, reminding me of central London, but even noisier. One thing that hits me is how straight the streets are. I can see buildings far into the distance, towering above the street. There are some familiar shops and coffee bars. I take a slow walk along the street, not venturing off into the side streets, as my sense of direction is not that great and I don't want to get lost. Steam is rising from the grilles in the street reminding me of films I have seen set in New York. I see a couple of burly policemen looking stunning in their uniforms, with big truncheons hanging at their side and between their legs from the look of the bulges in their pants. I smile politely at them as they walk past me and they smile back. After a few hours of wandering around the shops, I buy a new shirt for myself and a tie for Bradley. A small present to thank him for bringing me on this trip. Then I head back to the hotel to wait for Bradley to get back from his meeting.

Bradley walks into the suite, still looking as handsome as he did when he left this morning.

'Afternoon, gorgeous, how was your morning?' he asks.

'Very nice, thank you, I had a wander around the shops outside and I brought myself this shirt.' I hold up the shirt to show Bradley as he walks over to me, feeling the cloth of the shirt.

'That's a lovely shirt, it will suit you,' he says, then gives me a kiss.

'I got a little present for you as well.'

'You didn't have to do that.'

'It's just a little thank you for bringing me on the trip.'

'Having you here is my pleasure.'

'Ah, that's lovely.' I hand Bradley a small bag with the tie in it.

'That's nice, it will remind me of you and this trip whenever I wear it.' He pulls me into his arms and kisses me deeply.

'Have you had any lunch?' he asks

'Not yet, I was waiting for you to get back.'

'Let's order something light and have it delivered to the room as we have the dinner later.'

'Sounds good to me.' I pick up the room service menu off the table and have a browse whilst Bradley removes his suit jacket and tie, undoing the first two buttons on his white shirt. Bradley phones and orders the lunch. Then he pulls me back into his arms and I feel his hard cock as he grinds it slowly against me.

'I'm looking forward to this evening.' My cock begins to stiffen as he leans and gently nibbles at my neck. The shivers running down my spine from the gentle bites.

'So am I.'

'I don't suppose you have a dinner suit with you for the awards.'

'No, I only brought a suit with me, I didn't realise it was a black-tie event.'

Bradley smiles at me 'I didn't think you would have one, so I took the liberty of booking you into the tailor store in the lobby. We can head down there after lunch.'

Still holding me tight to him, Bradley stares into my eyes, with no words spoken. I'm sure he is feeling the same warmth that I am as we both look deeply into each other eyes.

When we met, he said he wasn't looking for a relationship, but standing here now, I think his thoughts have changed. I know mine have. I can't think of anything better than spending more time with Bradley. He makes me feel so secure and loved.

'Thanks, babes, I wouldn't want to seem out of place or embarrass you,' I say breaking the intense silence between us.

'You will never embarrass me.' He gives me another kiss as there is a knock on the door; the lunch has arrived.

Bradley opens the door for the waiter and he wheels

in a trolley, unloading the food onto the table in the room. Bradley had ordered another bottle of pink Prosecco, as he knows I like it a lot. Bradley tips the waiter as he leaves and we sit at the table to eat lunch. I'm still amazed by everything as I look out the windows over the skyline of New York, eating lunch in the five-star suite.

After we finish lunch, Bradley changes into some casual clothes and we head down the tailor store.

'Good afternoon,' the assistant says as we walk into the store.

'Afternoon, we have a booking in the name of David.' The assistant looks down list in his book on the desk.

'Ah, yes, which one of you is David?' he asks, his eyes giving us both a once over glance.

'I'm David.'

'How can we help you today?'

'He would like a black dinner suit with a purple bowtie,' Bradley replies before I can speak.

'Okay,' he says, then walks towards me from behind the counter, pulling a tape measure from around his neck. 'Let us get some measurements.' Bradley takes a seat and smiles at me as the assistant begins measuring my waist and chest. I blush slightly as his hand brushes against my balls when he measures my inside leg. I can see Bradley holding back laughter at my reaction.

The assistant begins rummaging through racks of black jackets and trousers along the wall. Returning to me swiftly with arms full of clothing. 'Please try these on for size,' he says, pointing to the changing room in the corner. I take the clothes and walk into the changing room, I have never worn a dinner suit. Taking off my clothes I put on the suit including a white winged collar shirt. I admire myself in the mirror looking very smart. Once dressed, I step back out into the store.

'You look amazing,' Bradley says as he stands and walks towards me.

'Thank you,' I reply feeling my face warming to his comments.

'The finishing touches,' Bradley says as he buttons the top of my shirt and ties a purple bow around my neck, adjusting it slightly as he stares into my eyes. 'Absolutely gorgeous,' he says and gives me a kiss. My face is burning hot now as my skin glows; I'm happy that Bradley is proud of the way I look.

'Yes, you're looking very fine, sir,' the assistant says.

'Thank you.'

'Okay, get changed,' Bradley says. I give him a smile and head back into the changing room, admiring myself once more with the bowtie on, I must get some photos later to show Mandy. I get changed and hand the clothes to the assistant who puts them into a suit bag and hands it back to me.

'Enjoy your evening, sir.'

'Thank you, I will.'

'Let's go,' Bradley says and we leave the store.

'Did we not have to pay?' I ask.

'No, that's all sorted,' Bradley replies.

We head back to the hotel suite. Once inside, I put the suit bag on the table. Before I can say anything to Bradley, he pulls me into his arms.

'You look so gorgeous in that suit, I want you now,'

he says, sliding his hands under my shirt, then down the back of my jeans, grabbing my arse cheeks. His cock is rock hard and he grinds against me for a while as he kisses me.

'Turn around and bend over,' he commands. I do as he says, placing my hands on the table. His hands wrap around me to undo my jeans, sliding them to the floor. I feel his face press against my arse through my briefs and hear him take a deep breath. He pulls my pants down and pushes his face into my arse, his tongue licking my hole making me wet. I moan and push back against his face as his tongue delves deeper into my hole. Closing my eyes, I'm lost in the pleasure of his tongue stretching and exploring my arse. His tongue leaves my arse and I hear him stand behind me. I can see his reflection in the glass windows as I watch him drop his jeans and underwear. As I feel his hard cock push into my arse, his full length slides deep into me as his hands grab my hips, pulling me back against him. I moan with pleasure, my cock hard, throbbing as he begins slow thrusts in and out of me. My hands slide on the table top as they begin to sweat whilst he fucks me.

Glancing at the windows, the sight of him ramming his cock into my arse turns me on more and I push back harder with every forward push of his cock. His speed increases and his breathing becomes louder as his cock slams into me like a jackhammer, until his final push forward as his cock explodes deep inside me.

'Turn around,' he orders, sounding breathless from the action.

He spits into his hand before grabbing my hard cock

and his own spent cock into his fist. He rubs his cock against mine, the pre-cum from my cock adding to lubricate as his hand begins vigorously stroking our cocks together. My hands grip the edge of the table as I begin to thrust into his fist, my breathing heavy and loud as I moan.

'Come for me,' he says in a deep, sexy voice. This sends me over the edge and my cum shoots from my cock, hitting my shirt and running between our cocks as he continues stroking them together. I buck wildly against his hand several times as I shoot my load, eventually I pull his hand away as my cock is too sensitive to take any more. Bradley pulls me tight into his arms and kisses me.

'That was great,' Bradley says.

'Sure was.'

'We best grab a shower.'

We share a shower together washing each other. Then we sit around in the suite in the hotel's white bathrobes, snuggling on the sofa, listening to some music until it's time to get ready for the awards dinner.

*A*fter a nice afternoon of snuggling together on the sofa, we both get ready for the dinner. Dressed in our dinner suits, Bradley ties my bowtie for me and I notice we have matching purple bow ties. He looks extremely handsome in his suit. Making me want to rip it off him again and have sex, but I control my urges.

'You look very gorgeous,' Bradley says to me as he finishes my bowtie.

'As do you, my handsome man.'

'I hope you enjoy this evening.'

'Just being here with you is wonderful. I hope you win an award; I'm sure you deserve one.'

'Thanks, I'm already a winner tonight, I have you.' Bradley says making me blush again.

'Are you ready to face the dinner?' he asks.

'As ready as I will ever be.'

'Good.' Bradley gives me a gentle kiss 'Let's go.'

We leave the hotel suite and take the lift to the

conference suite. As the lift doors open, we are met by a large queue of people waiting to enter the conference hall. I sneak a peek through the opening of the doors and can see the tables are decorated in black and gold. Bradley sees Robert and Michelle in the queue, so he heads over to them as I follow behind.

'Evening, have you seen Daniel?' Bradley asks Robert.

'I think they are already in the hall, we are on table six; I have checked the seating board.'

'Great, it should not take too long to get inside.'

'Evening, David, you're looking very dapper tonight.' Michelle says. I must have blushed slightly at her compliment.

'Thank you, you're looking stunning yourself,' I reply, she is wearing a long, gold, shimmering dress, something you normally see women wearing at the Oscars. We only queue for a few minutes and enter the hall. The place looks amazing. Tables dressed in black and gold fill the floor. There must be at least fifty tables, each seating eight people. At one end is a large stage, which has two huge video screens, one on each side, and a podium in the centre. Sparkling lights against a black curtain cover the wall behind the screens. We walk through the tables to find ours. Daniel and Susan are already at the table and they stand up to welcome us. Susan gives me a kiss on each cheek. Then we all sit down at the table.

There is a programme of the evening events on the table, so I pick it up and have a read. Eight awards are listed for various businesses, including one for best holding company. A waiter arrives and offers us a choice of red or white wine, which he pours for us. Another couple arrives at the table, who everyone seems to know, as they stand and greet them.

'This is David,' Bradley says gesturing to me, 'and this is Nicholas and Jenny.' He introduces them to me. 'Nicholas is the head of acquisitions for the US.'

'Very nice to meet you,' I say as I shake Nicholas's hand and give Jenny a couple of kisses, following Bradley's lead. We all sit down again and I look around the hall as Bradley talks work briefly with the others. Minutes later, the waiter returns, placing a starter of smoked salmon in front of us. The conversation ends as we eat the meal, the food is a delicious four courses, I am stuffed by the time the waiter offers us coffee. I feel Bradley's hand slide along my leg, as I look at him, he gives me a smile.

'Are you ok?' he asks.

'Yes, I'm enjoying the evening.' He gives me a little wink and squeezes my thigh. Once we finish eating, the lights in the hall dimm as a man walks onto the stage. Standing in the spotlight, music begins to play, and the man sings the opera song *Nessun Dorma*. I recognise it from TV. His voice is amazing and the emotion he puts into it brings a tear to my eye. He gets a well-deserved standing ovation at the end of the song. Next, a woman dressed in a flowing white dress comes onto the stage and thanks the singer before introducing herself and welcoming everyone to the awards ceremony.

She presents four of the awards, the nominees appearing on the large screens for each award. After the fourth winner collects their award, she introduces the next act to perform in between the awards. To my surprise it is a Celine Dionne tribute act. I sit awe struck as I watch her perform singing the classic *My Heart Will Go On*. This evening gets better and better. Celine gets another standing ovation. Then the woman comes back on stage and begins the introductions for best holding company. My heart skips a beat when Bradley appears on the huge screens, talking about his company's success. I slide my hand under the table and grab his hand, holding it tight, waiting for the announcement of the winner, wishing it will be him.

'The winner is...' It seems like forever before she says the name. 'Bradley Franklin.'

I scream loudly and clap, getting a little over excited that Bradley had won. Bradley takes me by surprise as I see us appear on the screens; he kisses my cheek as he stands up to go and get the award. Everyone in the hall would have seen him kiss me and my face go bright red. But I carry on clapping, standing up with everyone at the table as we watch Bradley accept his award. I'm so pleased for him and it is wonderful to be here with him as he wins. Bradley returns to the table with the crystal award and gives me a hug.

'You brought me luck,' he whispers in my ear as he kisses me again.

'Well done, I'm so proud of you,' I say as he hands me the award whilst the others congratulate him. After everyone had said well done to him, we all sat down again to watch the last three awards. I could see in Bradley's expression that he was very pleased he had won. After all the awards were presented, a large part of the stage slides back away from the tables, revealing a dance floor, and a DJ comes onto the remaining part of the stage. Playing various songs as we all chat around the table; a buzz of excitement at Bradley winning the award can be felt around the table as various people come over to congratulate him. The Champagne begins to flow as the night progresses. The DJ plays one of my favourite Kylie songs and I begin tapping my feet under the table.

'Why don't you have a dance?' Bradley asks.

'Are you going to dance with me?'

'I'm not the best dancer, but I would love to dance with you.'

We get up from the table and head to the dance floor; several couples are up dancing. We join them on the floor and jig around to the music. Bradley is right, he is not a great dancer, but neither am I, but it is really nice dancing with him. After a couple of songs, we both go back to the table and continue chatting with the others. Michelle catches me in conversation and is telling me how happy Bradley has seemed since he met me, which is really nice to hear. Another hour or so pass, then the slow songs begin to play, highlighting the end of the evening.

'Come and dance with me,' Bradley says, grabbing my hand and pulling me towards the dance floor. He holds me tight as we slowly move around the dance floor. 'Thank you for coming on this trip with me,' Bradley says, his voice slurring from the drink.

'It has been fantastic, a shame it has to end.'

'Well the weekend has to end, but you and me doesn't have to,' he says, catching me by surprise.

'What do you mean?'

'I would like to get more serious with you, how do you feel about being my boyfriend?'

'You have had too much drink,' I reply with a laugh. Bradley stops moving and grips my arms, looking me straight in the eyes.

'I know what I'm saying, I enjoy every minute I spend with you and I want to spend many more, will you be my boyfriend?' he asks again, his voice still slurring, but this time with a serious growl to it.

My heart skips a few beats as I reply, 'I would love to.'

Bradley kisses me and hugs me tight. 'Shall we head back to the suite now?' he says.

'Yeah, let's head back.'

We walk back to the table to say our goodbyes to everyone. Bradley hugs everyone and thanks them for coming to the awards, then he picks up the award and hands it to me to carry. We leave the hall and head back to our suite. Once we are in the suite, I put the award on the table. Bradley is swaying from the drink, so I help him into the bedroom and sit him on the bed so I can begin undressing him.

'You're gorgeous,' he says.

'You've had way too much drink tonight.'

'Maybe, but you're still gorgeous.'

Having removed his jacket and shirt, he collapses back onto the bed and I remove his shoes and socks before undoing his trousers, pulling them off with his pants. I stand and look down at him, his handsome tanned body looking lovely, his cock soft and laying in his thick pubic hair. But I'm not getting any action from that tonight.

I leave him lying on his back whilst I undress myself. Once I am naked, I get onto the bed and wake Bradley so he gets into the bed properly. He snuggles up behind me and falls back to sleep. I snuggle against him and hold his hand close to my chest. Falling asleep with those words ringing in my ears, will you be my boyfriend?

I wake up alone in the bed, stretching my legs. Bradley is not beside me. Staring up at the ceiling, my mouth is dry from the drink the night before. I wonder if Bradley really meant what he said last night or was he really drunk. I can hear voices mumbling in the lounge, I lay still. trying to hear what is being said, but they are talking to quiet, then I hear the door to the suite close.

Bradley comes back into the bedroom pushing a trolley, he is wearing a white bathrobe. 'Morning, gorgeous, how are you feeling today?'

'I'm not sure yet, I haven't moved my head much. I had way too much Champagne last night. How are you?'

'On top of the world,' he says with a smile. 'I have breakfast for you, if you are up to eating.'

'It might make me feel better.'

'Good, sit up.'

I shift on the bed and prop the pillows behind me, so

I am in a sitting position. Bradley pulls a tray with legs from the bottom of the trolley and places it over my legs. He puts a plate on the tray with a glass of juice. Lifting the silver cover off the plate, it had a full English breakfast on it.

'A special treat for my boyfriend,' he says as he leans down and kisses me. I blush a little with a mixture of excitement and relief; he had actually meant what he said. 'Did you think I wouldn't remember last night?'

'I have to be honest, I did think you were just drunk,' I say, feeling slightly embarrassed now that I thought that.

'We've been hanging out together for six months now and I really do enjoy your company, so why not make it official?' he says. 'Hopefully you want the same.'

'Yes, of course I do.'

'Good.' Bradley kisses me again, then picks up a glass of juice off the trolley and sits next to me on the bed. 'Eat up.'

I eat the breakfast whilst Bradley sits drinking his juice. Once my plate is cleared of food, he gets off the bed and puts the tray back onto the trolley. Walking back to the bed, he undoes the bathrobe, revealing his naked body, his cock already semi hard.

'So, boyfriend, let's make this official,' he says with a cheeky grin.

He drops the robe to the floor and climbs on top of me, pushing the quilt off the bed he gets between my legs, lowering himself onto me. My cock responds, stiffening as his cock rubs against it. His hands support him as he looks into my eyes. 'You're gorgeous and you bring out the best in me,' he says. Lowering his head, he gently bites my nipple, just enough to cause pain that turns me on, I moan and try to grind against him. Kissing across my chest, he bites the other nipple.

My hands hold onto his head as he trails kisses down over my belly, slowly working his way down to my cock. His tongue flicks over the head as I close my eyes and push up towards his mouth. Taking my cock between his lips, he slides the foreskin back off the head, then takes me fully into his mouth. Pushing down on his head, my breathing quickens as I slide my cock in and out of his warm, moist mouth.

His mouth moves down my shaft to my balls, which are already tight against my body, as I'm near the point of no return. Sucking my balls for a while, his tongue moves to my hole, gently licking before pushing his tongue into me, making my arse relax. He shifts up between my legs on his knees, holding my legs in the air. I feel his cock press against my hole, gently pushing only the head of his cock into me and withdrawing it. I reach up and squeeze his nipples hard, turning him on, he pushes his cock deep into me, pulling my legs against his chest, my feet resting against his shoulders as he fucks me. He breathes deeply against my foot, then licks along my foot to my toes, taking them in his mouth as his rhythmic fucking gets faster.

I'm lost in ecstasy, his tongue sliding between my toes, his cock deep inside me, I squeeze my own nipples hard. The pleasure overtakes my body as my cock shoots thick cum onto my belly. This sends Bradley over the edge as he drops my legs and grabs onto my shoulders, pulling my body against him, making his thrusts go deeper into me. A few harder fucks and he roars out, holding his cock deep inside me, I feel it throbbing as his cum shoots into me. He collapses onto me, my cum sticking our bodies together as he kisses me deeply.

'That was fucking great,' he says once he regains control of his breathing.

'Sure, you can fuck me anytime now, boyfriend,' I reply with a laugh. It seems funny calling him boyfriend.

'Don't worry, I will make sure I keep you satisfied,' he says, rolling to the side of me.

'I'm sure you will,' I say, shifting to kiss him as I run my hand through his thick chest hair. 'I'm all yours.'

We snuggle up together in bed for a while before getting showered and packed, ready to head back home. I can't wait to tell Mandy all about the weekend and the exciting news about me and Bradley. The journey to the airport and flight home are as luxurious as the journey to New York. We both have Champagne to celebrate our future together.

I'm looking forward to spending more time with Bradley and hopefully more travelling. He is such a wonderful man and I am falling in love with him. I wasn't expecting this when I met him, but I couldn't be happier.

13

Christmas

Sitting on my sofa in just my boxer shorts, silence around me, I'm thinking about Bradley. Things between us are going great. Returning from New York with him as my boyfriend was fantastic. Since we got back, I have been going to his place every weekend and we chat on the phone every day during the week when we're both working.

I could not be happier; now I have someone in my life to care about, I've realised what was missing deep down. That close, loving affection shared between two people and how it makes you feel inside. Bradley has gotten into my head and my heart. I didn't think I would ever let anyone get that close since my last relationship broke down. But here we are, both enjoying every minute we get to spend together.

It's Christmas Eve Usually, I don't look forward to

the festive season, spending time alone in my flat or out at friends' houses, most of them couples and madly in love with each other. This year Bradley wants me to spend Christmas with him. I'm off work from after my shift today until the day after Boxing Day and will stay at Bradley's. He has invited his sister and her family for Christmas Day. Bradley said I could invite a few friends if I wanted, but to be honest, I'm happy enjoying the time with him, and meeting his family will be stressful enough.

Like mine, Bradley's parents have both passed away, he only has one sister, Helen. She is married to a guy named Stuart and they have two young children; Albert, age fourteen, and Lucy, age eight. I have never met them before as they live near the Lake District. I'm kind of nervous about meeting them, but Bradley has tried to assure me they will adore me. I hope I get along with them.

Switching on the radio, *The Power Of Love* plays, one of those songs that bring back memories of past Christmases. It seems all they play on the radio this time of year is Christmas songs. Sitting still as the words of the song linger in my ears, taking me back two years to when I was with my ex, Craig. I close my eyes and see flickering images pulled from my memory, his face smiling at me as we sit in our PJs beside the Christmas tree in my flat, opening presents. He was the first man I truly loved; I gave him my heart, and he ripped it apart. The closer I got to him, the more he abused our relationship.

I lost count of the times he cheated on me, then begged my forgiveness or turned things around on me, blaming me for not having sex with him often enough so he had to get it from other guys because he had a higher sex drive.

I took years to see what he was really like, by which time my own self-esteem was battered and I had no self-confidence. I used the last of my strength to tell him to leave and not come back. He left me broken and unable to trust guys not to cheat on me, my confidence at an all-time low, that's when I gained weight eating to comfort my aching heart. The thought of ever meeting someone else never really entered my head until I met Bradley. The song ends, and I snap back to reality. Wiping a tear from my face, I look at the clock and jump up; I will be late for work if I don't get a move on. I'm heading straight to Bradley's after work to start our Christmas festivities. I'm rushing around the flat, getting dressed and ready for work, as *Driving Home for Christmas* blasts from the radio. I grab my bags, which are already packed with everything I need at Bradley's place, and the Christmas presents. Switching everything off in the flat, I head off to work.

The day seems to drag as the phones are quiet; people are too busy doing their last-minute shopping, I expect. I have a laugh with Mandy and the girls, chatting about our Christmas plans. We are closing early today and 4pm cannot come soon enough for me. When I have time to get Mandy on her own, I give her a little present. She tells me I shouldn't have, but I know she is secretly pleased. Mandy is my replacement mum, we hit off from the first day I worked here. Mandy is so happy that things with Bradley are going so well and she keeps hinting at wedding bells, not that it will happen anytime soon.

The end of the day finally arrives and we all say our goodbyes for the Christmas break. Mandy gives me a big hug and kiss on the cheek.

'You have a fantastic Christmas, kiddo,' she says.

'You too, babes, I hope you get everything you want.'

'I'm sure I will, see you after Christmas,' she says as she walks away.

I grab my bags from under my desk and leave the office, singing the song *Driving Home for Christmas* to myself as I walk along. Not that I'm driving, but there is something about the song that gives me the feeling the festivities are about to begin.

I arrive at Bradley's and knock on the door. He doesn't come to the door straight away so I knock again, this time a little louder.

'Merry Christmas, gorgeous,' he says as he opens the door.

'Merry Christmas,' I reply, walking into the hallway as he closes the door behind me and I drop my bags on the floor.

'Come here,' he says, grabbing my arm and pulling me into his arms. I love the immediate affection he gives me whenever we meet; it makes me feel adored and wanted. Hugging me tight, his lips press against mine. His tongue delves deep into my mouth as his hands run up my back and I melt into his arms as we kiss passionately.

'I've been waiting for you to arrive all day,' he says in between kisses. I feel his hard cock pressing against my leg, causing my own to stiffen. 'I have been feeling horny all day.' He gives me one deeper kiss before pulling away from me.

'Come with me.' Bradley takes my hand and leads me towards the basement door. It's been two weeks since we've been to the basement room, but I know how he likes me to behave down there. I follow him down the stairs to the softly-lit room. The lamp is switched off; today the room has several candles around the place, flickering light against the walls. Classical music is playing in the background. I notice the shelves of sex toys are open.

'What does Sir want today?' I say in a low, whimpering voice. Bradley does not reply; he leads me over to the bed.

'Lay face down on the bed,' he commands.

I do as I'm told and clamber onto the bed, face down still fully clothed. In the sex room, I do whatever Bradley wants, and I love his dominating side. He pulls my left hand to the corner bedpost and I watch as he ties a leather strap around my wrist, pulling it tight. I wince in pain as the strap catches my skin. Knowing not to speak, I bite into the pillow as he walks around the bed and pulls my right arm to the post and straps it tight.

Bradleys walks to the end of the bed and removes my shoes and socks. Then he climbs onto the bed and straddles me, his hands sliding underneath me as he undoes my jeans. Pulling my jeans off, he then removes my boxer shorts. Leaving me with my hands strapped to the bed, wearing just my shirt, my bare arse open to him. The anticipation of being fucked by him builds inside me as my cock stiffens against the bed.

Looking behind me, I can see him undressing. He strips off his clothes and his cock is already hard. He climbs back on the bed between my legs and I feel his soft hands sliding along my inner thighs, tenderly brushing against my skin. His hands meet at the top of my thighs, then he softly squeezes my balls. Pleasure flows from my balls to my cock as he plays with them. Pulling my now hard cock from under my body, he pushes my foreskin back off the head, twisting it in his fist as pre-cum leaks from my cock. His hands then slide over my arse cheeks, pulling them apart, I feel his breath as he blows delicately against my hole before his wet tongue licks around it, causing me to moan. I bury my face into the pillow to stifle any noise I may make.

Bradley clambers off the bed and I watch him as he walks to the shelves. I see him slide his leather gloves on, then he picks up a thick, eight-inch dildo and a smaller one, covering them in lube before walking back towards the bed. He climbs back on the mattress between my legs and I feel him rub the large dildo against my hole a few times, then he pushes it deep into me. He twists it as he pulls it out, then pushes it back into me, stretching my hole with every twist and thrust. I moan with pleasure as he fucks me with the dildo. He pushes the full length into me and holds it deep inside with his left hand. His right hand lifts my foot to his mouth and I feel his tongue lick between my toes. My cock leaks pre-cum as he twists the dildo against my prostate. His tongue licks down the sole of my foot, then returns to my toes, sucking them in his mouth. I bury my head further into the pillow so he cannot hear my moans of pleasure as he fucks me with the dildo.

Bradley shifts on the bed and I feel him pull the dildo out of my arse, then he rubs his own cock against my gaping hole. Moving his legs to the outside of mine, he grips my legs tight together as he forces his cock into my arse, his hands pressing down on my shoulders as he thrusts his cock faster into me, holding it deep inside. I feel his pubic hair rubbing my arse as he grinds his cock. After fucking me for a while, he shifts position again, pushing my legs wide apart with his knees. I hear a humming noise, then I feel the smaller, vibrating dildo slide into my arse. He holds it in position as he slides his cock into me, stretching my hole to take him and the dildo. The vibrations against my prostate make my cock shoot cum onto the bed, my whole-body quivers as the immense orgasm ripples through every muscle

Bradley thrusts fast and deep the vibrations sending him over the edge too, and as his cock throbs deep inside me, he roars out loud as his load shoots into me. He pulls his cock and the dildo out of me before he collapses onto my back. I can feel his cum leaking out of my hole, running over my balls and onto the bed. Bradley breathes heavy in my ear.

'Merry Christmas, my gorgeous man,' he says as he tries to catch his breath.

I turn my face and kiss his cheek. 'Merry Christmas, Sir.'

Bradley lies on me for a while, then gets off the bed and unties my hands. I roll onto my back, away from the wet patch on the bed. Bradley leans down and kisses me.

'We best get things ready upstairs before the family arrive,' he says.

'Okay,' I reply as I get off the bed.

Bradley pulls me into his arms again, giving me a long, lingering kiss. 'I'm glad you're here for Christmas.'

'I wouldn't want to be anywhere else.'

'Good,' he says as he smacks my arse hard, then jumps away from me so I can't get him back.

'You will pay for that.'

'Maybe,' he says as he gets dressed. I put on my clothes and we head back upstairs. Bradley locks the door to the basement, just to make sure his family don't go down there.

'Would you like a drink?' Bradley asks.

'Yes, please, something alcoholic.'

'Pink Prosecco, then.'

'Sounds great, I'll put my bag upstairs whilst you get it.'

When I come down the stairs, I pick up my bag of presents from the hallway. Bradley is sitting in the lounge; there is a very large real Christmas tree, elegantly decorated, in the corner of the room, with various shaped presents placed around the bottom. The smell of the tree hits my senses, reminding me of Christmas when I was a kid, coming home to find the tree standing in our lounge. I place my presents under the tree, ready for the morning.

I sit next to Bradley and he hands me my drink. 'Did you decorate the tree?' I ask. Bradley's look says it all, he had obviously paid someone to decorate the tree.

'Cheers, here's to our first Christmas,' he says, raising his glass, trying to distract me from the question. We clink our glasses together.

'Cheers.'

Bradley puts his glass down and heads over to the tree. Rummaging through the presents, he picks one and brings it back.

'Here you go,' he says, handing me the present.

'Isn't it too early for presents?'

'Never too early, this is a special Christmas Eve gift for my gorgeous man,' he says as he leans in and gives me a kiss.

'You should have told me, I haven't got you a gift for tonight.'

'I never give to receive and it is nothing outstanding, so please open it.'

'Thank you,' I reply as I eagerly unwrap the present, trying to imagine what this special gift could be.

Inside is a Christmas jumper, black with a huge snowman on the front a large carrot nose sticking out.

'It's lovely,' I say, giving him a kiss.

'Christmas jumpers; my sister always insists we all wear them on Christmas day. I have one,' he says with a smile.

'Very thoughtful, thank you.'

Bradley leans over and kisses me again.

'My sister said she should arrive about 9pm, the bedrooms are ready for them. I'm looking forward to you meeting them.'

'I'm a little nervous, to be honest.'

'Stop worrying, they will love you,' he says then drinks the rest of his Prosecco. 'Let's get ready, as they should be here soon.'

*W*e are standing in the kitchen when the doorbell rings. A shiver of anxiety runs down my spine.

'That's them. Are you ready to meet the family?' he says, giving me a big hug.

'Ready as I will ever be.'

I follow Bradley to the front door, excited and nervous, standing behind him as he opens the door.

'Bradley,' Helen calls out and rushes forward, hugging him tight. She is a little smaller than Bradley, with long, flowing, dark brown hair and olive-toned skin similar to his. She then looks towards me. 'You must be David, I have heard so much about you.' She lets go of Bradley and gives me a hug. Bradley is shaking hands with Stuart, a tall, thin man with pale skin and well-groomed hair. Then I watch Lucy run to Bradley; he sweeps her off her feet, lifting her into the air. She looks like a miniature version of her mother

'Hey, Squirrel, how are you?' Lucy lets out a very

infectious giggle as Bradley gives her a hug. I shake hands with Stuart. The last one into the house is Albert, a skinny boy with long, dark hair, dressed entirely in black, clearly going through the gothic stage of teenage life. Bradley puts Lucy down and says, 'Come here, Albert.' Bradley pulls him into his arms. A small smirk on Albert's face gives away his appreciation of the affection from Bradley.

'Come in, make yourself at home,' Bradley says, scooping up one case as Stuart grabs the other.

Lucy skips off into the living room and screams, 'Mummy, come and look at the lovely Christmas tree.'

Helen walks to the living room door. 'Oh, Bradley, it is beautiful.'

'Thank you,' he says, not mentioning that some else had dressed the tree.

'Why don't you take the cases upstairs; you know where the rooms are. Me and David will organise drinks, what would you like?' Bradley asks

'Okay, then we can catch up. I will have a red wine, please,' Helen says, walking towards the stairs, leaving Stuart to carry the cases.

'Same for me, please,' Stuart says.

Albert and Lucy have already taken seats in the living room.

'So, what do you think of them?' Bradley asks as we get to the kitchen.

'They seem nice so far.'

'Great,' he says, then gives me a kiss.

Bradley pours two glasses of Prosecco for us and

wine for Helen and Stuart. 'Could you ask the kids what they would like to drink?' Bradley asks.

I walk back to the living room and find them both sitting on the edge of the sofa in silence. 'What would you like to drink?'

'Could I have an apple juice, please?' Albert asks.

'Me too,' Lucy says.

'Okay.' I smile at them and head back to the kitchen, helping Bradley with the kids' drinks. He puts all the drinks on a tray and carries it into the living room. Picking up our drinks, we sit on the other sofa. 'Help yourself,' Bradley says to Albert and Lucy.

'Play Christmas selection,' Bradley says using his voice commands to activate the music. *Last Christmas* plays around the room. I ask them if they are looking forward to opening their Christmas presents and Lucy chats away about all the things she would like for Christmas as Albert sits in silence. After a while, Helen and Stuart come back into the room. Picking up their drinks, they shift the kids off the sofa and sit down; Lucy squeezes back in between them and Albert sits on the floor. The chat turns to me as Helen kind of grills me about my life in a subtle way. I could tell she was only concerned about Bradley and who he was getting involved with. Once we had broken the ice, the conversation flowed as the Christmas music played in the background.

Having had a long journey down in the car, they wanted to go to bed and the kids wanted to sleep as they know it's Christmas Day tomorrow—present time. We all head up to bed.

15

*B*radley's room is at the top floor of the house. He lives in a town house with three floors and the basement. His bedroom is luxurious with a huge king-size bed covered in a pure white silk duvet. Mirror wardrobes all along one wall give the illusion the room is double its size. The bedside cabinets are mirror effect and there is a large silver statue of a naked male on the mirror cabinet at the end of the bed. The light is a huge crystal chandelier and the whole room shouts glitzy. There is an elegant, large en-suite bathroom through another door. He had converted two rooms into one large space for himself.

As I close the bedroom door, I feel Bradley press against me from behind, his hands sliding around my waist as he pulls me back into his body. His voice in a whisper as his breath warms against my ear as he says, 'Merry Christmas.' He tenderly bites my ear lobe, then drags his tongue across the back of my neck, kissing me lightly. My body melts into his arms as I moan with pleasure. Turning me to face him, he pushes me back against the door, grabbing my hands, entwining his fingers between mine as he lifts them above my head, holding them tight against the door. His lips meet mine, dry and soft, he kisses me, then bites my lower lip, sending pain and pleasure tingling through my body. He kisses and bites down the side of my neck, and I moan as my cock stiffens with each bite.

He releases my hands and grabs my T-shirt, pulling it off over my head. My nipples are hard and my hairless body feels the cool of the room as his mouth moves to my right nipple, licking it, teasing it between his lips, making it stiffen more before blowing against it. The coolness of his breath makes me shiver. His hands slide down the back of my jeans, grabbing my arse cheeks as he continues biting my nipple. My breath gets heavy as my cock feels wet in my pants, straining hard against my jeans, begging for release. He moves away just long enough to remove his own T-shirt, then pulls my body tight against his. The hairs on his chest brush against my smooth skin as his tongue explores inside my mouth. Our tongues entwine in synchronicity as we kiss. Bradley breaks away and kisses down my chest and belly as he gets down on his knees, his hands delicately trailing down my body, tracing where he has kissed.

My cock is throbbing now, leaking as I know my release is coming. He tugs the belt loose on my jeans. My hands brush through his hair as he undoes my jeans and slides them to the floor, leaving just the wet cotton material of my pants between his mouth and my cock. His fingers slide up the back of my legs seductively, my cock throbbing, aching for his wet mouth to take it deep into his throat. Pushing under the material of my pants, his hands grab my arse, pulling my pants tighter against my cock. He drags his tongue along the length of my cock, tasting my pre-cum through the wet cotton. He breathes deeply against my cock, then bites the head through my pants.

I moan more with every bite as he teases my cock, causing it to leak heavily. My hands pull tight on his hair as my body loses itself in ecstasy. His hands grab my pants and pull them down from the back, causing the waistband to drag my cock down before is springs free, my foreskin fully retracted, the head wet and dripping. I feel his lips touch the head, desperate to be in his mouth. I pull on his hair, forcing his mouth along my length as I let out a pleasurable moan when his nose presses against my belly, my cock in his throat as I grind against his face.

Thrusting into his mouth, my legs shake as my orgasm takes over, my hands grab his head tight as my cock throbs in his mouth my cum shooting deep into his throat. He continues sucking and licking my cock until I have to pull his head away. Bradley stands and kisses me intensely, the taste of my cum shared between our mouths. He undoes his jeans and pushes them down, his cock hard and glistening. I capture glimpses of our bodies in the various mirrors around the room. He turns me around and I place my hands above my head on the door. I feel the head of his cock push between my arse cheeks as he runs his fingers smoothly down my spine before his hands grab my hips. I bite my lip as he rams his full length into me. He follows this with slow, deep thrusts, his pubic hair brushing against my arse with every forward thrust. His hands slide around my front and I feel his fingers squeeze my nipples hard, making me push back against his hard cock. It doesn't take him long to reach his climax. A few deeper thrusts, then he holds his cock fully in me as I feel his cum shooting deep within me. The hair on his chest rubs against my back as he pulls me into his body. His breath is heavy on my neck.

'Merry Christmas, handsome,' I say as I turn to face him. We kiss once more.

'We best get to sleep; the kids will undoubtedly be awake early in the morning,' Bradley says.

'True, that includes me. I can't wait to give you my presents. Let's get to sleep.' I give Bradley one last kiss, then we both remove the clothes from our feet and snuggle up in bed, swiftly falling into a deep sleep.

I'm woken by the sound of the kids jumping around downstairs. Bradley is snuggled up behind me and I can feel his semi-erect cock twitching against my arse.

'Morning,' he whispers. His breath warm against my ear.

'Morning, handsome.' I snuggle back against him, pulling his arm tight against my chest.

'It sounds like the kids are awake. We best not keep them waiting, as Helen will not allow them to open any presents until we're all there.'

'Two more minutes, please?' I say pushing back so his cock is forced between my cheeks. He moans softy and pulls me tighter against his chest.

'Okay, two minutes, then we must get up.'

We lay snuggled in the bed, his breath blowing on the back of my neck as he breathes.

'Do the kids open all their presents early?'

'No, Helen lets them choose one present to open, then they open the rest this afternoon, after we have finished dinner.'

There is a knock at the door. 'Uncle Bradley, are you awake?' Lucy calls through the door.

'Yes, Squirrel, we will be down in two minutes.'

'Okay, there's lots of presents under the tree. Santa has been here,' she says with a giggle to her voice. We hear her footsteps head back down the stairs.

'We best get up before she comes back.'

Giving Bradley a long, lingering kiss before I climb out of bed, looking in the mirrors around the room. My cock is hard from snuggling with Bradley. We both put on our PJs and head downstairs.

'Morning, boys,' Helen says as we get to the bottom of the stairs. 'I have made fresh coffee, would you like one?'

'Yes, please, Sis.'

'I'd love one as well, thanks.'

Helen walks to the kitchen and I go into the lounge. Lucy jumps up and runs into Bradley's arms.

'Look at all the presents,' she says. Seeing her so excited is great.

'Wow, you must have been a good girl this year,'

Bradley says, playing along with the Santa story. She hugs him tight. a huge smile on her face. 'Morning Stuart, how did you sleep?'

'Pretty well, thanks. The bed is very comfortable,' he says, sitting on the sofa in his PJs with Albert next to him.

'Good, I'm glad to hear.'

We sit on the other sofa across from Stuart and Albert, Lucy snuggles in between me and Bradley as Helen returns with the coffee.

'That bed is so comfy, you must give me the details of where you got it,' she says, handing us our coffees.

'Remind me later and I will dig it out for you. I think our little Squirrel wants a present.'

'Yes, yes,' Lucy screams as she jumps up from the sofa, almost knocking my coffee out of my hand.

'Okay, choose a present,' Helen says.

Albert also jumps up, the first sign of excitement I have seen from him. The two kids rummage around under the tree, checking the labels on the presents, taking their time to select the one they want. Albert is too old to believe in Santa, but he is not spoiling it for his sister, which is nice. It has been a long time since I've spent Christmas around children and it's heart-warming to see the excitement they have, but then I can't wait to get my presents and give Bradley his.

We watch the kids as they sit on the floor near the tree and unwrap the presents, Albert cautiously pulling the paper off, whereas Lucy is just ripping it off as quick as she can. She screams as she sees the gift, a set for making jewellery, jumping up from the floor and running over to her mum to show her.

Albert had chosen a large box, unwrapping it to reveal the latest Xbox console. A huge smile stretches across his face as he opens the box. 'Can I use your TV, please?' he asks Bradley.

'Yes, of course. Show theatre.' Bradley says, using his voice commands to activate the TV

The panels in the wall move and the large TV screen glides into the room. Albert doesn't seem surprised; he must have seen the way the TV appears before. Bradley gets up from the sofa and helps Albert connect the console to sockets in the wall and within minutes he's playing a video game. Lucy's sitting on the floor playing with her jewellery set.

We all sit around in our PJs, chatting as the kids play. This truly is a family Christmas. After about an hour, Helen tells the kids to get dressed, so we all head upstairs to shower and dress for the day. It's Christmas jumper time.

16

*B*radley pulls his jumper over his head as he stretches it out. A reindeer with a flashing red nose is in the centre of his chest.

'Do you like it?' he asks, smiling at me.

'Yes, it's lovely,' I reply with a little laugh.

'Sorry, it is family tradition. Helen won't be happy if we don't wear them.'

'It's okay, breaks the ice to be honest. Shall we see what they are wearing?'

'Okay, come here first.' Bradley pulls me into his arms, hugging me tight as he kisses me.

'Come on,' he says, pulling me by my hand to the door. We walk downstairs. The kids are both playing in matching jumpers with flashing presents on the front. They must have been chosen by Helen. Stuart is looking uncomfortable in a bright blue jumper with a large Santa face on the front. Helen has a big flashing Christmas bauble on hers.

'Yeah, David, good to see you're in the jumper club,' Helen says with a big smile.

'All part of Christmas,' I reply not mentioning that Bradley had got it for me.

'Why don't you fix us some drinks, Bradley, whilst I start the dinner, Buck's Fizz would be nice,' Helen says.

I give Bradley a puzzled look.

'You know I cannot cook. Sis always cooks Christmas dinner.'

'You're terrible, Bradley, inviting your Sister for Christmas then getting her to cook.'

'Well, we could have all had burnt offerings if you wanted.'

I tut at his reply. 'Would you like any help, Helen?' I ask.

'Thanks for offering, but I'm okay, cooking for six is not much different from cooking for four.'

'Okay, well, if you want any help, just give me a shout.'

'You're a sweetie,' she says, giving me a kiss on the cheek as she heads off to the kitchen.

I help Bradley make the drinks, then we return to the lounge and watch the kids play, leaving Helen in the kitchen preparing dinner. Conversation between Bradley and Stuart changes to work and I rapidly realise that Stuart is in charge of the UK distribution for Bradley's company. Helen returns to the lounge after about an hour, breaking the conversation.

'Talking work again, boys? I'm sure David doesn't want to hear about that,' she says, giving me a sly smile.

'Yes, sorry, dear,' Stuart says.

'So, David, tell me about how you won my brother's heart?'

'Helen, that's not what I said,' Bradley says with an abrupt tone.

'You need not say it, Bradley. I can see it in your eyes.'

'Well, I'm sure Bradley has told you the gory details.' I say, drinking the last of my Buck's Fizz.

'I'm just teasing you both. You make a lovely couple and it's good to see Bradley interested in something other than work.'

'More drinks, anyone?' Bradley says, getting up from the sofa, trying to avoid any more quizzing from his sister.

Bradley returns with another tray of Buck's Fizz. Helen changes the conversation, and we chat about their home in the Lake District and she invites us to go there when we are free. After two hours of Helen popping in and out of the kitchen, she announces dinner is ready. We all go into the dining room and even I'm surprised how beautiful the table is set.

'Bradley, the table looks fantastic did you arrange it?' I ask already expecting him to say someone had done it for him.

'Some things are better done by others with the right skills,' he replies with his bright, white smile.

'Well, it is wonderful.'

The food had been placed on the table by Helen so we could help ourselves, and she had already filled plates for the kids. We all sit down and Bradley opens some Champagne. There is little conversation whilst we eat dinner, which tastes great. After dinner, Bradley tells Helen and Stuart to sit in the lounge whilst we clear away the plates and load the dishwasher.

Once everything is cleared away, Bradley grabs me into his arms. 'Are you having a nice time?' he asks quietly.

'Yes, it's lovely.' His lips meet mine and his hands slide underneath my jumper, stroking my lower back as he kisses me. I pull him tighter to me, exploring his mouth with my tongue.

'I'm glad. Well, it is present time now; I hope you like your gifts,' he says.

'I hope you like yours, I don't have the money you have, so they are not extravagant gifts.'

'David, it's not about the value of a gift, it is the thought going into it that matters.'

'Yes, my thoughts too. I hope you like what I have got you.'

'Having you here with me has already made this the best Christmas ever.' He kisses me before I can answer.

'Come on, let's watch the kids open the rest of their presents,' he says as he smacks my backside playfully.

'Okay.' I give him one last kiss and then we go back into the lounge.

'Thank you for a wonderful dinner, Helen,' I say.

'My pleasure, David. Well, kids, it's present time. Sort the presents and hand them out please.'

Albert and Lucy sort through the presents without hesitation. They hand me three presents and hand the others their presents. I read the labels on mine; two are from Bradley and one from the others. We all open our presents. I get a tie from Helen and Stuart, Bradley has gotten me a silver bangle, which I had mentioned to him a while ago, and some of the aftershave I liked from the hotel in New York. My presents to Bradley are a glitzy mirror picture frame with a picture of us at the gala dinner in New York and a silver tie pin that will remind him of me when he wears it. The kids got at least fifteen presents each, and none of them looked cheap. Helen and Stuart had brought each other jewellery. We spent the rest of the evening chatting and drinking Champagne until we all headed upstairs. It was a wonderful Christmas day and one I will remember for many years to come.

Bradley closes the bedroom door and turns the lock to make sure the kids can't get in the room.

'It's been a lovely day. I have enjoyed every moment,' I say with a slight slur to my voice from all the Champagne.

'Yes, I love having you around,' Bradley says, sounding as drunk as me.

We both undress and get into bed naked. Bradley snuggles up behind me; wrapping his hand around my waist, he pulls me back against him, his cock snuggled against my arse. We must have both been tired and drunk, as we fell asleep within minutes of our heads hitting the pillows.

Bradley is behind me, so I move back against him,

feeling his hard cock against my arse. I wriggle about so it slides between my cheeks.

'Morning, gorgeous,' Bradley says with a sleepy voice.

'Morning, handsome.'

Bradley slides his hands around my belly and pulls me back into him. His cock throbs and stiffens more as he starts to slowly thrust against my hole. His tongue licks the back of my neck trailing across to my ear lobe as he shifts his body so he can push his cock deeper into me. My sweaty arse takes his full length with ease. I moan as his pubic hair rubs against my arse and his thrusts quicken as his nibbles on my ear. I push back with every thrust he makes into me, taking him as deep as I can, his breath warm against my wet ear. I slide my hand backwards over his arse, pulling him against me. He pushes me onto my front and climbs on top of me, thrusting his cock deep into me, his hands sliding under my chest squeezing my nipples hard. I have to bury my face into the pillow to stifle my moans of pleasure so his family doesn't hear. My cock is hard from rubbing against the bed and pre-cum leaks onto the sheets. Bradley pulls his hands from under me and places them on my shoulders, holding me to the bed as he thrusts harder into me. The sound of his body slapping against mine echoes around the room. He is nearing the edge as I hear him growling as his pace quickens before one last push into me and his cock throbs as his load shoots into me. He collapses onto my back, his wet, sweaty chest rubs against my back as he pants heavily in my ear.

'What a nice way to wake up,' he says in between his breaths.

'Sure is,' I reply.

Bradley rolls me onto my back and straddles me, looking down into my eyes. He grabs my hands, pushing them up above my head, and holds them to the bed, lowering his face close to mine, keeping eye contact all the time. He looks as though he is about to say something, but changes his mind and kisses me instead. As he pulls away, he stares into my eyes again. He's so close I can feel the warmth of his breath against my face.

Lost in the moment, I take a deep breath. 'I love you, Bradley,' I whisper. The words leave my mouth before I can stop them. The silence seems like a lifetime as his eyes look deep into mine.

'I love you too,' he replies. 'I have for some time now.'

'Really?' I say with a nervous giggle.

'Yes, really.'

Bradley kisses me deeply, our tongues dancing together between our mouths.

'We best get up before the Squirrel comes knocking,' he says.

'Okay, handsome.'

Bradley shifts off me and climbs off the bed. I watch his lovely arse as he walks towards the bathroom. I have a huge smile on my face; this gorgeous man truly is mine. When he comes out of the bathroom, I get up and use the bathroom, then we both get our PJs on to go downstairs.

Helen is already downstairs with the kids in the lounge.

'Morning, boys, would you like coffee?'

'Yes, please. Where is Stuart?' Bradley asks.

'He is just packing away our things. We have to leave soon, as it is a long drive back.'

'Sorry, I didn't realise the time,' he says.

Helen goes off to the kitchen, Bradley and I sit on the sofa in the lounge. Lucy jumps in between us and cuddles Bradley's arm.

'Have you had a nice time?' I ask Lucy and Albert.

'Yes, it has been fantastic,' Lucy replies enthusiastically before Albert can speak.

'Yes, it has been very nice, thank you, Uncle Bradley, and it was nice to meet you David,' Albert says. He is definitely mature for his age.

'It was lovely having you here, me and David will have to come and visit you next year.' Bradley says as Helen walks back into the room with the coffee.

'Yes, you should come up, you know you're welcome anytime.'

'We will, I promise,' Bradleys says as Helen hands us our coffee.

Stuart comes into the room. 'All packed and ready to head off,' he says.

'Okay, let me finish my coffee,' Helen snaps at him.

'I wasn't trying to rush you, just saying we are ready when you are.'

We drink the coffee then say our goodbyes to them all. Helen gets a little tearful as she hugs Bradley; I can tell how close they are. Lucy hangs onto Bradley as long as she can before Helen pulls her off him and sends her to the car. I give Helen a kiss, and she whispers in my ear to take care of Bradley. We both stand on the doorstep and wave them off as the car pulls away from the house. Stepping back into the house, Bradley shuts the front door.

'Peace, at last,' Bradley says with a sigh.

'They are great. It was very nice spending Christmas with them.'

'Yeah, I know. Come here.'

Bradley wraps his arms around me, tenderly kissing me, his tongue exploring my mouth. Then he pulls away a little, rubbing his nose against mine.

'I love you, mister. We have a good future to look forward to,' Bradley says in a quiet, soothing voice.

'I love you too,' I say, kissing him back.

Hugging each other tight, we have gone from a no strings relationship to falling in love this year. I wonder what next year will bring for us?

17

February

I switch on the rainfall shower, allowing the water to heat as I look at myself in the mirror wall. Bradley's bathroom is like something out of a five-star hotel, every detail matched to perfection. I step into the shower area; there is no enclosure, the sloped floor drains the water away without it flooding the bathroom, dark grey tiles cover the walls around the shower area. The hot water cascades onto my skin, causing it to prickle with the heat, steam rising from the floor as the water hits the cool tiles.

Facing the wall, I close my eyes and lean my head back, enjoying the water as it massages my smooth body. Bradley's hand slides around my waist and pulls me tight against his chest, the hairs rubbing against my skin as an approving moan leaves my lips.

"Morning, sweetheart," I say as I slide my hands down his thick, toned thighs.

"Morning, gorgeous," he replies. His tongue traces across the back of my neck.

I lean my head to one side and he kisses my neck as he grinds himself against me, his cock stiffening between my legs. His hands slide from my belly up to my chest; his fingers brush over my already hard nipples and I moan as my body trembles from his touch. The kisses turn to gentle bites as he takes my nipples between his thumbs and index fingers. Squeezing hard, he sends pleasurable pain deep into my chest. My cock is hard, the skin pulling away from the head, the stabs from the water against it making me thicken to my full length.

He twists my nipples between his fingers, making me push back onto him, his mouth and fingers teasing me. I have to turn and face him.

"I need to get work by nine," I say, kissing him, my tongue exploring his mouth.

"Okay, we can save this until tonight, but then you're all mine," he replies between kisses.

"Always."

He reaches for the shower gel. Pouring it into his hands, he lathers my shoulders, moving his hands over my chest and belly, cleaning every inch of my smooth body.

"Turn around."

I do what he says and his hands lather my back, sliding down to my arse. His fingers slide between my cheeks as his other hand cleans my cock and balls. He pulls my skin back hard as he cleans my shaft and I let out gasps of pleasure. He knows how much that turns me on.

I grab his hand to stop him. "Later, I will be late for work."

"Okay, spoil sport," he says with a laugh.

We finish showering together, then head to the bedroom to get dry and dressed. Bradley slips on a bathrobe; he's working from home today.

"I will head down and make breakfast," he says, giving me a quick kiss.

I get dressed for work; I have left a few clothes at Bradley's place now as I often stay over at least one night during the week. Using his aftershave, I spray my neck generously before heading down to the kitchen.

Bradley had put toast and juice on the table for me. I walk over to him and give him a kiss.

"You smell nice," he says.

"Thanks to you, babes," I reply with a cheeky smile and sit down at the table. Bradley finishes the coffee and brings it over, taking a seat opposite me.

"So, what are we doing for Valentine's?" I ask before biting into my toast.

"I've told you already, it is a surprise."

"You won't even give me a little clue?"

"No, so you may as well stop asking. You will never get it out of me."

"Who is the spoil sport now?" I smile at him across the table.

"You will pay for that later, mister."

"Promises, promises," I laugh, although my cock stirs at the thought of what he might do later.

"I will be here about eight tonight as I'm meeting Brian for a quick drink after work. He reckons I must have been kidnapped by you as he hasn't seen me out for so long."

"No problem, I have a lot of work to do so that should work well with my timings. We can get a take away."

"Great."

We finished eating breakfast before I had to leave for work. Bradley hugged me tight and gave me a lingering kiss before I left the kitchen, making me want to stay with him for the day.

"Have a good day, gorgeous."

"You too, sweetheart," I give him one last kiss, then head off to work, grabbing my bag from the hall cupboard as I leave the house.

I rush through the office door, reaching my desk with two minutes to spare before my start time. Harry, my manager, gives me a glare from the other side of the room. We work in an open plan office, rows of desks with advisors chained to the phones, monitored constantly, they even monitor how long we spend in the toilet. Mandy finishes the call she was dealing with and takes off her headset.

"Morning, another night with Bradley?" she asks.

"Yes, babes, it is so hard to leave him when I know he is working from home."

Mandy laughs. "You have changed your tune, things must be getting serious?"

"Nah, it's his cock I hate leaving," I reply, trying to laugh off her comment.

She gives me one of her knowing looks. Mandy has known me far too long for me to get away with hiding things from her. Harry suddenly appears at our bank of desks.

"Mandy, you have been unavailable on the phone over four minutes. Save the personal chat until lunchtime," Harry snaps at her.

"Sorry, Harry," she says, putting her headset back on. She sets her phone to available and a call comes through. "Good morning, Mandy speaking, how can I help you?"

"David, you should be available by now," Harry says with his normal grumpy voice. I don't reply but give him a fake smile as I put my headset on. Harry turns and walks away, towards his desk. I give Mandy a cheeky smile and she sticks two fingers up at Harry behind his back.

The three hours to lunch seem to fly by as the calls come in fast and furious, people moaning about the cost of insurance all morning. A message pops up on my screen to warn me it's lunchtime, so I finish my call, then log out of the phone. Mandy was on the same lunch break as me, so we headed out of the office to get something to eat and a little fresh air. After sitting at a desk, not being able to walk about all morning, you need to escape the office.

We head to a little café nearby and get a coffee and sandwich, sitting at a small table in the corner.

"So, answer my question from earlier, are things getting serious?" Mandy asks before I can even take a bite out of my sandwich.

"Honestly, I'm not sure, after Craig I didn't think I would ever fall for someone again. You know how much he hurt me and the mess I was in when it ended."

"David, you can't keep dwelling in the past. Otherwise it will ruin your future. Yes, Craig was a bastard and out of order for the way he treated you. But from what you've told me, Bradley is not like him at all."

"No, he isn't. The sex with him is great and the way he treats me, gives me special, warm feelings inside. You know, when your tummy goes all funny."

"Well, take the next step, why don't you suggest moving in together so you can spend more time with him. He obviously makes you happy, I haven't seen you this happy in years."

"I don't know, Mandy, what if spending too much time together makes it all go wrong?"

"If that's the case, it's better to know now, rather than another year down the road. Stop stalling, talk to him, and tell him how you're feeling and see what he thinks."

"I suppose you're right, I'm just nervous I remember what happened with Crai—" Mandy thrusts her hand towards my face.

"Stop," she shouts before I can finish his name. "Bloody forget Craig, he's gone, that part of your life is over. Enjoy your time with Bradley, he sounds like the right man for you."

I laugh at her reaction, she reminds me of my Mum giving me advice. We chat away about work and our lives, it's rare we get a lunch break together due to our shifts.

I glance at my watch. "We better head back or Harry will jump up and down."

Mandy laughs. "Yes, he will get even grumpier than he was this morning," she says, laughing more.

We get up from the table and head back to the office. On the walk, she tells me again to go for it with Bradley. The afternoon goes as quick as the morning; the phones have been busy lately. Mandy was on an earlier shift so she had already left by the time I finish. Breathing a sigh of relief, I put my stuff into my bag and head off to meet Brian at the pub.

It's been months since I have been to this pub, the last time I was here was the night I met Bradley. Walking in the door, the familiar eighties music is playing and the place is virtually empty, with only a few guys sitting around. Brian's already sitting in the corner. When he sees me, he jumps up and screams, running over. We kiss each other once on each cheek and hug.

"Hey, sweetie, you're looking well," he says in his high-pitched camp voice.

"Ah, thanks, babes, it's lovely to see you. Let me get a drink, I need one after today. Do you want one?" I ask.

"I've got one, thanks, sweets."

"Okay, grab a seat and I will be over in a minute," I say, as I walk over to the bar and order a large house red. Sitting down at the table with Brian, I take a big gulp of the wine.

I let out a loud gasp. "That feels better."

"We have so much to catch up with, last time I saw you was when you had just got back from New York," he says.

"I know, babes, how time flies when you're having fun," I smile and wink at Brian. He laughs at me.

"So, tell me all, are you still seeing that beefcake, Bradley?"

"Yes, he is such a wonderful guy, we have been seeing each other nearly nine months now."

"Congrats, sweets, well, I've got news for you, I met a guy named Pete two months ago and we're still fucking like rabbits." He screams with laughter. "He is meeting me here later, so you might catch a peek at him before you head home."

"Oh, babes, I'm so pleased for you, looks like we have both found decent guys at last."

"I'll drink to that, cheers." Our glasses clink together and we have a drink of wine. I tell Brian all about Christmas at Bradley's and meeting his sister and family. He fills me in on the graphic details of how he met Pete. Time flies by as we chat away, waiting for Pete to arrive.

A huge smile spreads across Brian's face as Pete walks in the bar. He is a good-looking guy, about six feet tall, with deep blue eyes and medium length blond hair. And he's obviously in the gym a lot from the size of his muscles. Brian stands up and gives him a hug and a long, lingering kiss.

"Do either of you want a drink?" he asks.

"Get us a bottle and we can share it, sweets," Brian says.

"I'm okay, thanks, babes. I need to head off soon; I said I would get to Bradleys about eight."

"Okay, back in a minute," he says, turning towards the bar.

"So, what do you think?" Brian asks.

"Very nice, he definitely looks like he works out."

"Yeah, he goes to the gym everyday. He's got the strength to hold me down," he says with a smile.

Pete came back to the table, so I used the opportunity to leave. Giving Pete a quick kiss on the cheek and Brian a long hug and two kisses.

"Catch up again soon, babes."

"Yes, maybe make it a double date, give Bradley my love."

"That sounds good, I will do. Bye." I wave and as I head out of the bar, I walk past The Crypt restaurant where Bradley and I had our first meal together. A warm glow builds inside me from the memories. Hurrying along to get to Bradley's place, I can't wait to see him.

nocking on the door, I wait for Bradley. He opens the door and he is wearing joggers and a T-shirt, but looks a sexy as ever.

"Come in, gorgeous."

I walk into the house and put my bag in the hall cupboard whilst he closes the front door. He pulls me into his arms, hugging me tight. His lips touch mine and his tongue traces along my lower lip and slips into my mouth. My eyes close, the warmth and security of being in his arms floods through my body. Whenever I arrive at this house, he always makes me feel wanted and loved.

"Grab a seat in the lounge and I will get you a drink."

Giving him a quick kiss, I kick off my shoes and head into the lounge, collapsing onto the large, comfortable sofa. Soft music was already playing in the background. Bradley comes back and hands me a glass of red wine, and sits beside me on the sofa.

"So, how was your day?"

"Work was manic; I'm sure the phones get busier every day. I went to lunch with Mandy today, which was nice, we had time to catch up."

"That's good, I hope she is doing well."

"Yeah, we put the world to rights as always. Then I met Brian at the bar, he is doing well, found himself a hunky blond guy they have been together two months."

"Sounds like you had a full-on day."

"Very. So, how was your day?"

"Video meetings with the US team, emails, all the routine things. I've ordered a pizza; it should be here soon."

"Great."

We drink our wine as we chat away about the day. The pizza arrives, so we sit at the kitchen table and eat, still chatting. I decide not to mention the chat with Mandy as I'm not staying this evening because Bradley is going to the US for two days and he has an early flight tomorrow. After the pizza, we head back to the lounge and get comfy on the sofa with more wine and listen to the music.

Bradley puts his glass on the side table, leaning into me, placing a soft kiss on my lips, so I put my glass down. He pulls me on top of him, so I straddle his legs, my eyes lock onto his lovely, deep brown eyes. His hands lightly touch the sides of my face and guide my mouth to his. Our lips touch and my eyes close as my body melts into the ecstasy of him; his tongue twists with mine, making me grind slowly on his lap. His hands move from my face and unbutton my shirt, tugging it free from my trousers as he continues kissing me deeply. His fingers trace along my belly, sending shivers through my skin as they move to my nipples, circling them, teasing me, they are aching for him to twist them hard between his thumb and index finger.

My moans are stifled by his mouth, as he squeezes my nipples hard, the pain spreading across my chest, causing my cock to stiffen. He continues to tweak my nipples, the mix of pleasure and pain making me grind faster against him, his cock stiffening as I push down into his lap. Twisting my nipples and pulling them away from my chest, the pain becomes overwhelming as my moans turn to growls, but I don't want him to stop. My cock leaks pre-cum. His hands move to my shoulders and slide my shirt off, pushing it to the floor. His mouth now kisses my tender nipples, sucking them between his lips. I lean my head back, lost in the frenzy of pleasure washing through my body, and I push my throbbing, hard nipple deeper into his mouth. He continues his onslaught. My cock is rock-hard and I'm rubbing it as hard against his body as I can, bringing myself closer to coming.

His hands move to my belt, tugging it loose. Undoing my trousers, his hands slide around my waist, then push down the back of my trousers. Grabbing my arse, he pulls me hard against him in rhythm with my thrusting. My breath is heavy and loud as my orgasm gets closer. He slides his fingers between my arse cheeks and pushes one deep into me as he bites hard onto my nipple. My cock explodes. I'm unable to hold back, thick cum shooting into my boxers as I collapse onto him, gasping for breath, my body quivering as load after load bursts from my cock. He kisses my neck, pulling his finger out of me, hugging me tight to his chest whilst the orgasm wanes.

Once I regain my composure, I lift myself off his chest and kiss him deeply.

"That felt fantastic," I say as my breath settles.

He kisses me back. "I'm glad. It's nice to give you pleasure."

"What about you?"

"I'm fine, you know I get what I want when I need it, tonight was for you, as I will be away for two days."

"You're so lovely," I reply, kissing him again.

"So are you."

I climb off Bradley and stand, then pick my shirt up off the floor and put it back on. He watches me and takes a sip of his wine as I button my shirt. I adjust my cock in my boxers.

"Yuck, my boxers are all wet."

"I'm sure it was worth it," he says with a smile.

"Always with you," I reply and sit next to him on the sofa, giving him a kiss before picking up my glass of wine.

We sit and chat for an hour until I head home so Bradley can get to sleep before his early flight. It's hard leaving him; I would love to spend every night sleeping next to him. Maybe we will get there one day soon.

19

I get home from another hectic day at work. It seems to get busier every day. Throwing the keys on the side, I close the door behind me. I don't enjoy coming home to the empty flat anymore, I would much rather go home to Bradley's place. Walking into the lounge, I switch on the CD player and my favourite disc plays starting with *On a Night Like This*. I walk to the bathroom, singing along to myself. Stripping off my work clothes, I throw them in the washing basket, and looking at myself in the mirror, I think I might have lost a little weight.

Switching on the shower, I step in under the stream of hot water, closing my eyes as the water pours like a waterfall onto my head, streaming down my body. I grab the shower gel and lather myself, cleaning away the stress of the day. Once I am clean, I switch off the shower and step out into the bathroom. Grabbing a towel, I dry myself and hang the towel over the rail.

I walk naked from the bathroom to the kitchen; I live

alone so I need not worry about someone seeing me. *Bad Romance* is now playing in the lounge and I sing along as I take one of my pre-made meals, this one is lasagne, out of the fridge and place it in the microwave. Switching it on, I have a little dance to the bedroom, my small, fat cock swinging about as I dance.

I slip on a pair of boxers and a T-shirt, running my fingers through my hair and pushing it back off my face. I walk back into the kitchen as the song changes to *I Feel Love*, another one of my favourites, so I sing along, waiting for the microwave to finish. With a loud ding, the food stops cooking I leave it to stand for two minutes, transferring it to a plate, and take it to the table in the lounge to eat. It doesn't take me long to eat the meal; I wash up the dishes and switch off the CD player. Sitting on the sofa, I switch on the TV and browse through the channels, trying to find something to watch. I decide on a reality TV programme, more for the noise in the flat than because I was interested in watching the programme. It's almost seven and I'm getting fidgety because Bradley said he would phone from the US tonight. I recline on the sofa, and my cell phone beside me rings. I look at the screen and Bradley's face is smiling back at me as I answer the phone.

"Evening, sweetheart."

"Hello, gorgeous, how has your day been?"

"Manic again. I'm not sure what is going on at work, but it gets busier every day. How're things going over there?"

"All well, thanks, we secured another company today that will boost profits soon."

"That's good to hear, I'm pleased its going well."

"Thanks, so where are you at the moment?"

"I'm in the flat, lying on the sofa, watching some TV."

"Sounds nice, what are you wearing?"

"Boxers and a T-shirt, where are you and what are you wearing?" I ask with an inquisitive tone.

"I'm in my hotel room, lying naked on my bed with a very hard cock."

My cock stiffens at the image in my mind of Bradley on the bed. "Sounds nice, I wish I was there with you," I say, the excitement obvious in my voice.

"Well, you're on the phone, why don't you get naked."

"Are you getting kinky with me, Bradley?"

"I'm naked and horny as hell, does that answer your question?"

He need not say anything else. "Hold on." I put the phone on the sofa and take off my T-shirt and boxers, my cock is now hard, the foreskin pulling back off the head, pre-cum leaking from the tip. I pick up the phone "I'm naked now, Sir," I say in a low whisper.

"Good, now put the phone on the loud speaker and place it on the sofa next to you," he says, I can hear his breathing changing and I know he is playing with his cock.

I do as I'm told. "The phone is on the sofa, Sir." My cock is twitching with excitement.

"Do not touch your cock until I say you can," he orders, "now squeeze your nipples hard and tell me how it feels."

I squeeze my nipples, rolling them between my thumb and finger, then twist them hard. I moan with pleasure, "It feels good, Sir, the pain is spreading through my chest, and my cock is throbbing and leaking," I say, my breath getting heavy as I continue moaning.

"Carry on squeezing them tight as I would if I was there, twist them and make them red raw."

His phone is on the loudspeaker as well and I can hear his breathing getting heavy. I continue twisting and pulling my nipples, squeezing them as hard as I can cope, and my cock is throbbing as pre-cum runs down the shaft. I want to grab it and thrust into my hand until I come, but Bradley hasn't said I can yet.

Panting for breath and moaning loudly as my balls tighten, I say, "I'm getting close to coming, Sir."

"I want you to cum at the same time as me, so hold back," he demands with a commanding voice.

"Yes, Sir."

Bradley's breathing is getting faster and I can hear the slurping sound of the lube as his hand furiously slides up and down his shaft.

"I'm almost there, now rub your cock hard," he says, panting for breath, a growl to his voice.

Squeezing my left nipple hard, I grab my cock with my right hand. I'm so close to coming it only takes a few strokes before I'm calling out to Bradley. "I'm coming, Sir." As the words leave my mouth, my cock explodes, thick streams of cum shoot onto my belly as Bradley roars down the phone, his load shooting over him. I relax on the sofa, my cock spent but twitching from the orgasm. I listen to Bradley breathing heavy, not saying a word.

After a few minutes, he breaks the silence. "I needed that."

"Me too, sweetheart. I miss you when you're away."

"I miss you too, gorgeous, but I will be back tomorrow."

"Good, I can't wait."

"Well, I best get cleaned up, I have another meeting to go to."

"Okay, sweetheart, enjoy the rest of your day."

"Sleep well, gorgeous, night-night."

"Night." A dead tone rings in my ear as he hangs up the phone.

I need to talk to him when he gets back about how I'm feeling. I clean myself up and head to bed, eager for tomorrow to come soon.

J rush out of work as soon as the clock hits five. Bradley is back from the US, so I want to get to his place and see him. He is always in my thoughts now; I want to spend as much time with him as possible. The nagging doubts caused by Craig still race around in my mind, and as I fear things could all go wrong between us, my insecurity brings me down.

I arrive at Bradley's and knock on the door, eager to see his lovely face. He opens the door and I'm greeted by his gorgeous, smiling face.

"Hello, gorgeous, come in."

I step into the house and he shuts the door behind me before swiftly pulling me into a tight embrace. His warm, soft lips touch mine and I close my eyes, all my insecurities fade when he holds me tight. He kisses me deeply, his tongue slipping between my lips, his hands sliding down my back and grabbing my arse. I don't know why I have any doubts about how he feels when he always greets me like this.

"I've been waiting for you to get here."

"Oh, yeah, why is that, my lovely man?" I say with a hint of seduction in my voice.

"Come with me and I will show you." He takes my hand and leads me towards the door to the basement; my cock stiffens and my body tingles at the thought of what he wants to do with me.

I follow him down the stairs. Soft music is playing in the background, the usual lamp in the corner is off, and several candles have been placed around the room and are giving of a soft warm glow as they burn. The smell of lavender from the candles hangs heavy in the air. The doors next to the sex swing are open, his various sex toys on display, everything looks familiar. I notice a chain hanging from the ceiling in the centre with leather cuffs attached to the end; something new to the room.

Bradley leads me across the room. Stopping, he positions me under the chain. "Stand here."

"Yes, Sir." In this place I become completely submissive to him. He is in charge in this room. I've never tried to disobey him here, I'm not sure how he would react if I did, not that I want to. One thing I love about Bradley is the way he dominates me in this room.

I stand still as he walks to the corner of the room. Picking up a red scarf, he walks back to me. Without a word, he folds the scarf and ties it firmly over my eyes. My other senses heighten and my skin prickles as I listen carefully, trying to work out where Bradley is in the room. I feel him unbuttoning my shirt. He doesn't speak. Pulling the shirt free from my trousers, he slips it off my shoulders. The cool air of the room hits my skin, making my nipples stiffen. He tugs at my belt, undoing my trousers, and he pushes them to the floor, along with my boxers.

I'm now standing naked under the chain, my trousers and boxers around my ankles, crumpled on top of my shoes. He grabs my right wrist and lifts my arm above my head, the leather cuff cuts into my wrist as he pulls it tight before doing the same with my left arm. Strapped to the chain, naked, my cock is throbbing, the cool air of the room blows against my leaking pre-cum. I've never been in this position before and my heart thuds deep in my chest, the anticipation of what is coming taking over.

I cannot hear Bradley; he must be moving very slowly and quietly. My body shivers and tingles as his fingers touch my shoulders, before tenderly running down my back, tracing over my spine, rubbing my lower back.

"Relax and allow your senses to take over," he whispers in my ear. His tongue traces over my ear lobe, the feeling of the cool air intensifies against the wetness on my ear. He has moved away from my body and I can hear him sorting through things in the corner.

The warmth of his naked body brushes against my skin and his cock presses between my legs.

"I brought a present back for you from my trip," he says in a low whisper, his voice still breathy.

He wraps his arms around my chest and something cold and metal in his hand touches my skin. My whole-body shivers with excitement as he hugs me tight and grinds his cock between my legs, nibbling across my shoulders. He disappears again, teasing me with his fingers. I feel them drag over my belly, he is in front of me now and he gives each of my nipples a squeeze, teasing them to stiffen.

His breath is warm against my ear. "These are for you," he says in a low growl. I can't hold back the moan of pleasure as the cold metal clamps snap tight onto my nipples. His mouth meets mine, and he bites my lower lip, pushing his tongue deep into my mouth, stifling my moans as he tugs on the chain between the nipple clamps, pulling on my swollen, hard, aroused nipples.

He pulls away from me and my body quivers with pleasure. I feel his mouth close over the head of my throbbing cock, his tongue sliding under my foreskin as it circles the head. Licking along my shaft, the nipple clamps squeezing tighter, my balls tighten as he uses his mouth skilfully to tease my cock. I try to use the chains to swing my body and push my cock deeper into his mouth, taking me to the edge. I growl noisily as cum shoots from my dick. He pulls his mouth away, allowing cum to hit the floor. My cock spasms as it shoots my load, the last of the cum hanging from the tip.

I hang from the chains, my body relaxing from the orgasm, I take a sharp intake of breath as a large dildo pushes into my arse and Bradley holds it deep inside me as my arse relaxes to its size. After a few minutes he moves it gradually in and out of me. Twisting it, he stretches my hole, getting me ready for his cock. He continues fucking me with the dildo, my arse trying to pull it deeper inside as I bite my lip to stop myself making too much noise.

Pulling the dildo out of me, I hear it hit the floor as his arms slide over my belly. Pulling me back against his body, his cock slides between my cheeks and deep inside me. He moans into my ear and grinds his pubic hair against my arse. Nibbling at my ear lobe, he thrusts in and out of me, his breath warm and heavy against my neck. "I've missed you," he says with a low growl as his cock settles into a gentle rhythm of fucking me. The chains above my head creak with each deep thrust he makes, rubbing hard against my prostate, forcing more cum to leak from my cock.

He grabs the chain attached to the nipple clamps and pulls it hard, a pleasurable pain shooting through my chest, and I push back hard on his cock. His thrusts get harder and deeper. I can't stifle my moans as his body slams against mine. He crushes me tight against him and thrusts forcefully into me, his breathing heavy. I can tell he is about to cum. Roaring loudly as his cock throbs deep inside me, his body bucks against mine as he loses control. Hugging me tight, he slowly grinds as his cock shoots the last of his cum. After a while he pulls his cock out of me, my arse still throbbing and gaping from his fucking.

He unties the blindfold and removes it and his eyes stare into mine. We don't speak; our feelings are shared between us through that deep stare. He reaches up and undoes the cuffs from my wrists and I collapse against him, panting for breath. He hugs me tight, the warmth of our sweaty bodies comforting.

"Welcome home, sweetheart."

"It's always nice to come home to you," he replies

giving me a gentle kiss. "Let's get dressed and go upstairs."

We head up to the kitchen and Bradley pours two glasses of red wine, handing me one.

"So, what do you fancy for dinner?" he asks.

"I'm happy with a take away, shall we order Indian?"

"Sounds good." He shuffles through some take away menus on the side, passing one to me. "What would you like?"

I have a quick browse and tell Bradley what I would like and he picks up the phone and calls the order through to the Indian take away.

"How was work today?" he asks.

"Okay, it's so busy at the moment I don't seem to have time to think, they seem to keep adding more to the job all the time."

"Oh, dear, not much fun."

"No, not anymore, so how was your day?"

We spend a while chatting in the kitchen until the take away arrives, we sit at the table and eat the food. It's delicious, just what I needed. I spend another hour with Bradley before heading home as I have work tomorrow.

"What time will you get here tomorrow evening?" he asks.

"About six-thirty, do I need to bring anything special for Valentine's night?" I ask, trying to get him to hint at what he has planned for Saturday.

"No, just bring yourself along."

"Okay," I reply pulling a sad face as I look at him.

"I'm not telling you what we're doing so you can give up the puppy dog face," he says with a laugh.

"Well, it was worth a try," I reply with a smile.

"I'm sure you will enjoy the day."

"Okay, sweetheart, I will wait patiently."

"Good," he replies, giving me a kiss goodnight.

I kiss him back and hug him tight. "Well, I better head off home."

"Okay, I look forward to seeing you tomorrow."

He follows me to the front door and we have one final kiss before I head home. It's getting harder and harder to leave him, I want to be with him forever.

21

*F*riday and the work week has finally finished. I'm at Bradley's for the weekend and Valentine's Day tomorrow. Already showered and changed, we head to the local pizza restaurant to eat. Walking downstairs, Bradley is already waiting at the bottom of the stairs.

"You look and smell nice and fresh."

"Thanks, you don't look so bad yourself." I give him a cheeky smile and he smiles back at me giving me a kiss.

We put on our jackets and leave the house, walking to the pizza restaurant, holding hands. Bradley had booked a table, so we are seated quickly, and there's only one other couple in the restaurant. It reminds me of my nights out with Craig as I watched the couple sat opposite each other at the table, not talking, just scanning social media on their mobile phones.

The waitress comes over and hands us menus and Bradley orders a bottle of wine.

"Are you okay? You seem quiet this evening," he says.

"Yeah, I'm fine, starting to chill out from the busy day at work," I reply and smile.

"Okay, as long as there is nothing wrong."

"Nothing."

He gives me a strange look, as though he knows something is not right. When the waitress returns with the wine, we order our pizza, a stuffed crust meat extravaganza to share and chat away about the day. My days at work are all very similar, answering phones, listening to people moan about things, so I always feel like I'm repeating myself to him, but he always looks interested when I talk about work. The pizza arrives and we both tuck in, eating half each. It's extremely nice and filling. We finish the wine and Bradley pays the bill; he never lets me pay when we're out and I've given up trying to convince him to let me pay as I only get the "business will pay" lecture.

After we have eaten, we take a slow walk home. I love the way he isn't embarrassed to hold my hand in public, all the time I was with Craig he never would in the street.

Getting home, Bradley gets a bottle of wine and two glasses from the kitchen and we sit in the lounge. He puts on some eighties music as he knows it's my favourite.

"Cheers," he says raising his glass, so I clink mine against his.

"Cheers," we both take a sip of the wine.

"So, tell me what's on your mind," he says.

"Nothing, I told you earlier."

"I know you better than you think, and I can tell there is something on your mind. The last few weeks you have looked like you were about to say something and stopped several times. Please tell me what you're worrying about."

Taking a large gulp of the wine, I take a deep breath. "I'm finding it harder to leave you and head home to an empty flat. I miss you when I'm away from you. I'm not saying we should live together or anything, I just don't enjoy being at my flat alone after I've had a lovely time with you."

"Whoa, that was confusing, you don't like leaving me and going home alone but you're not suggesting we live together?"

"I'm scared about us living together," I blurt out the words before I can stop them and tears well in my eyes as I stare at him and all the pent-up feelings overwhelm me.

He puts his glass down. "Come here," he says pulling me into him and hugging me tight. Tears stream down my face and I sob into his shoulder.

"I'm sorry," I struggle to speak between sobs, "I'm being silly."

"You're not silly, tell me what you're scared about?"

I shift back away from him so I can look at his face. "I don't know where to begin."

"Just say it, David, you can tell me anything."

I take another deep breath, trying to stop myself

from crying. "The only guy I have lived with was my ex, Craig. We were together for over four years. After two years of living together, things changed, he disappeared for nights. Returning home, he'd tell me he had stayed at friends because he needed space from me, putting me down and making me feel dreadful about myself." Bradley doesn't speak but nods in acknowledgement and grips my hands tight as I speak, his eyes glued to mine. "He did that for six months. After that, I found out he had been cheating on me with guys he met on nights out. When I confronted him about it, he even turned that against me, blaming me for not having sex with him often enough, so he had to get it off other guys. Eventually I told him to leave, but it left me destroyed with no self-esteem. I took a long time to get to a point where I could go out again. Now I've met you and I've fallen in love again, I'm scared of getting hurt."

I stare into Bradley's eyes, his eyes searching deep within mine. It seems like a lifetime before he speaks.

"David, I will never hurt you." His voice is strong and calm, the honesty emanating through his words. "You should have told me about this a long time ago and I could have reassured you."

"I didn't know how to bring it into a conversation," I reply my voice still shaky.

"No one can predict the future, but I see my future with you. I wasn't looking for love when we met, but in the months we have been together I have found my soulmate in you."

His words make me more emotional. "I love you, more than words can say."

"I love you too, now stop worrying about the past, the future is about us now."

"Okay." I hug him tightly and give him a lingering kiss.

"Come on, let's go to bed, it's Valentine's tomorrow and we will have a lovely day."

We kiss before heading up to bed. Snuggling together, Bradley holds me tight, his warm body pressed against me from behind, his legs entwined with mine. I am happy and secure as I drift off to sleep.

———

I wake up alone in the bed, Bradley must be downstairs. Stretching out across the bed star-shaped, the silky duvet slides over my smooth skin as I lift my arms towards the ceiling. I'm happier now. I have told Bradley my fears and I think he understands. I hear him coming up the stairs, the sound of a piano playing *Flashlight* getting louder as he gets closer, and watch the open door waiting for him to appear. He walks in the room, carrying a tray, all he is wearing are a pair of black silk boxers with little love hearts over them, his lovely, toned, hairy chest looking as wonderful as ever.

"Happy Valentine's, gorgeous," he says with a big smile across his face.

"Happy Valentine's, sweetheart."

He walks to my side of the bed and places the tray on the bedside table. Two glasses of Buck's Fizz sit either side of a small box of chocolates placed on top of a card. Rose petals are scattered over the silver tray, a small portable speaker playing the song. It reminds me of the night we met and our meal in The Crypt restaurant.

"What a romantic way to start the day," I say and he leans down, giving me a lingering kiss.

"A romantic day for the most important man in my life."

My heart flutters deep in my chest and my face burns as I smile at him. "You're so wonderful, I'm so lucky to have you in my life."

"We are both as lucky as each other," he replies clambering onto the bed, kissing me as he climbs over me to the other side. We both sit up in the bed. "Pass my drink, please."

I hand him his glass and we clink our glasses together.

"To us," he says, taking a sip of his drink.

"Yes, to us," I reply, sipping mine, "where did you get this version of the song?"

"I asked the musicians from the restaurant to record it for me."

My eyes well up, my body tingling at the thought he had gone to so much trouble. "It's lovely," I try to say as my voice trembles, a tear rolls down my face.

"Don't cry, it was meant to make you happy, you're a soppy sod."

"I am happy, nobody has ever done anything like this for me," I reply, crying and laughing, my emotions all over the place.

He leans over and gives me a kiss. "I love you and I will do anything for you."

I put my glass on the bedside table and he does the same. Straddling me, his fingers touch the sides of my face and his eyes look deep into mine. I can see the passion flickering deep within him. His lips soft as they press to mine, I close my eyes and allow him to take control as his tongue slips into my mouth and he kisses me. He pulls the duvet from between us, the silk of his boxer shorts glide over my cock as he grinds into my lap.

His hands are soft and gentle as they slide down my arms. They reach my hands and our fingers entwine. He continues kissing me. Pulling his tongue from my mouth, he delicately bites my lower lip and chin and as he bites the soft skin of my neck I feel my cock stiffening.

"I'm going to make love to you," he murmurs between kisses and bites to the side of my neck.

His nose nuzzles against my ear lobe as I melt into his body. Our cocks rub together through the silk of his shorts. Moving down the bed, he grabs my legs and pulls me down so I'm lying flat on my back. He kneels between my legs, pushing my thighs apart as he leans down, planting soft kisses onto my hard nipples.

I lift my hands off the bed and run my fingers through his hair as his tongue lovingly teases my nipples. My cock is leaking as the silk of his boxers rubs over my cock head. My eyes still closed, I let out a low moan as his tongue traces between my nipples.

Feeling him pulling away from me, I open my eyes to watch him and he looks down at me. "You're so fucking gorgeous," he whispers with a heavy breath as his fingers trace down from my shoulders, giving my nipples a quick twist before continuing down over my soft belly. He lifts my legs at the knees and pushes my legs further apart. Letting out a moan of approval as he looks at my hard cock, my balls tight against my body, he traces his fingers down the sides of my balls and pushes them between my arse cheeks and my body shivers as they rub over my hole. My arse is sweaty from the night's sleep, allowing his fingers to push into me with ease.

I watch him pull his cock out of his boxers; he is fully erect. Adjusting his position, he slides the head of his cock between my cheeks, easing it into my hole. My arse is ready and aching to have him deep inside. He leans down and kisses me as he pushes deeper into me, my moans of pleasure stifled by his mouth. His cock slides in and out of me and I push my feet into the bed, lifting my hips in rhythm with his thrust. He shifts back onto his knees, grinding himself deeper into me. Fucking me harder, he grabs my hips, pulling me towards him as he pounds my arse faster.

I grab the sheets and moan noisily, losing myself in pleasure, His growling gets louder as he fucks me faster I can tell he is about to cum. I grab my hard cock and rub it vigorously. As he roars, he holds his cock deep in me, shooting his cum. My cock explodes, thick, warm cum shooting over my belly. He continues grinding into me as his cock comes, panting for breath, his head and chest sweating. When his orgasm is over, he collapses on top of me, breathing heavy in my ear, my warm cum gluing our sweaty bodies together.

"Happy Valentine's again," he whispers in my ear between his gasps for air.

I hug him tight to my body. "Happy Valentine's, sweetheart."

We lay together for a while before taking a shower together. Once we are clean, I grab his Valentine's card out of my bag and we both sit back on the bed to open the cards, finishing our Buck's Fizz. His card is lovely, the words reiterating his love for me as mine did for him. Getting dressed, we head down to the kitchen and Bradley makes us breakfast. We spend a few hours at the house, chatting and sitting about together.

"Okay, we better head out for your Valentine's surprise," Bradley says.

"Valentine's surprise? You mean there's more?"

"Today is a special day and I want to make it special for you."

"So, where are we heading?"

"Get your jacket and shoes; we'll take a walk down to the river."

"Okay."

Within minutes we are out of the house and walking down through Trafalgar Square, towards the river. We continue walking towards Westminster, walking past Big Ben and over the bridge towards the London Eye.

"So, have you worked out where we are going yet?" he asks with a smile.

"A restaurant along the river?" I try to guess.

"No, we are having lunch on the London Eye."

"Really," I scream, jumping with excitement, I've never been on the Eye.

"Yes, really, I said I wanted to do something special today."

171

I hug him tight and give him a lingering kiss. "You are amazing."

He laughs at me. "We best get moving, we have to be on time to get into the capsule." Grabbing my hand, he pulls me along and we rush to the entrance gate. Bradley hands a ticket to the young man at the gate and he lets us through. We wait about ten minutes for an empty capsule to glide into the boarding area with a table set for two. Two of the staff rush into the capsule, placing a metal tray with a cover over it in the middle of the table, as well as a bottle of Champagne. They exit the capsule as quick as they entered and the young man gestures us into the capsule. He closes the door, and capsule begins to lift into the air.

Not only are we having lunch on the London Eye, we also have a capsule all to ourselves, this is amazing. Bradley opens the bottle of Champagne and pours us a glass each, handing one to me first, picking up the other one.

"To our first Valentine's of many," he says, clinking his glass against mine.

We both have a sip of the Champagne and he puts his hand around my waist, standing next to me, as we look out of the capsule while it rises into the air. It's a lovely, crisp, clear day and the view over London is amazing. The capsule remains level as we reach the highest point before it starts the decent down the other side.

"Do you think we should eat the lunch?" I ask.

"Not yet. We get to go around three times, so there is

plenty of time to eat. Besides, I have another surprise for you."

I give him a puzzled look. "What else could you surprise me with?"

Bradley looks me deep into my eyes and takes my left hand, my body trembles, my hand shakes as he gets down on one knee. His other hand rummages in his jacket pocket.

"Oh my God, oh my God," I repeat, my voice shaking.

"David, I love you with all my heart. Will you marry me?" He pulls a small ring box from his pocket and holds it out.

My eyes well up again and I'm shivering all over, my heart thudding in my chest. After all my doubts I cannot believe he is asking me to marry him. I seem to have lost control of my voice as I watch him down on one knee. The voice in my head is saying yes but the words are not coming out.

"Well, will you?" he asks. This time his voice is shaking.

"Yes, yes," the words finally escape from my mouth as I take the box from him.

He stands up and hugs me tighter than he ever has before, kissing me hard. Breaking away so I can open the box, I find that the inside is a silver-coloured ring with four stones that resemble diamonds set into the band.

"Do you like it?" he asks

"I love it, I like silver jewellery."

"It's platinum and they are real diamonds."

"Wow, it must have cost a fortune," I say, shocked by what he has said.

"Cost is irrelevant when it comes to you, my lovely man," he replies. "Well, put it on."

I take the ring out of the box and slide it onto my finger, amazingly it fits perfectly.

"Happy Valentine's, my fiancé," he says, kissing me again.

"I love you, Bradley." I wrap my arms around him jumping with excitement as I kiss him back, my heart still thudding hard in my chest.

"You know this means you will have to move in my place with me."

My emotions overwhelm me again as tears roll down my cheeks. "Do you mean that?"

"Yes, of course, I want you with me every day."

I hug him tight. "This is the best Valentine's Day I have ever had."

"Well, now I hope you will relax and enjoy our time together."

"I will, I promise." I give him another long, lingering kiss.

"We better not let the lunch go to waste."

"True."

We sit down at the table and remove the cover from the lunch revealing a platter of various meats and cheeses. Bradley pours more Champagne, and we both eat. I chat away excitedly about moving into Bradley's place and getting married. My heart slowly returns to a normal beat. I know he promised me a surprise, but I'm in total shock from his Valentine's surprises.

I can't wait to tell Mandy and Brian this news. We're getting married. We enjoy the lunch and the rest of the ride on the London Eye before heading home. This has been the best Valentine's ever.

22

*I*t has been three weeks since Bradley proposed on the London Eye and asked me to move into his house. Since then, my life has been a whirlwind of decisions, including big ones; like, should I sell my flat or just rent it out?

Bradley has companies that deal with property rental, so he suggested using them to rent the flat and look after it for me. He said property prices are still on the increase in London, so it's best to hold on to it for now as it will earn me money. He will always be a businessman at heart.

The day I move to his house has arrived and I feel a little strange and hesitant, it is a big step as we learn to live with each other. They say you don't really know someone until you live with them and that is true. I couldn't have guessed what Craig, my ex, would turn out like when we moved in together. Mandy keeps telling me off for comparing this move to living with

Craig, but I can't help that those emotions are bubbling up from time to time.

I'm startled by a knock at the door. Opening the door, I'm greeted by two burly, hot men. Both wearing cargo pants and T-shirts that cling to every well-toned muscle in their bodies. Their arms look like they deadlift weight in the gym all the time.

"Hi, are you David?" the biggest guy asks.

"Yes."

"Alright, I'm Martin, this is Andy. We're here to move your things," he says holding out his hand. I grip his hand and shake it.

"Great, come in."

We walk to the lounge where I have stacked everything I'm taking to Bradley's place. All my furniture is staying at the flat as it is being rented out furnished.

"It's just this stack of things here," I say, giving Martin a smile.

"Okay, mate, it won't take us long to clear this lot." He has a real gruff East London tone to his voice, which is sexy. I like real manly guys.

"Shall I give you a hand?"

"We'll be fine, mate, thanks."

"Okay." I step out of their way and watch them pick up the boxes with ease and take them out of the flat.

Within fifteen minutes, all my things were removed from the lounge. All that was left was just Martin standing staring at me; Andy must have stayed in their truck.

"If that's everything, mate, we'll drop it off at the address on the sheet," Martin says then leaves the flat.

"Thanks," I raise my hand and give him a wave.

Staring around, the place feels weird, although it still has my furniture in the rooms. All my personal bits and pieces have been removed, leaving the place feeling more like a showroom than a flat. My heart sinks a little as I will miss this place, but on the plus side, I will get to spend a lot more time with Bradley. I have one last look in the hallway mirror and smile at myself. Picking up the keys, I lock the door behind me and take a walk to Bradley's place. I suppose I should stop calling it Bradley's now as it will be my home.

By the time I get to the house, the guys had dropped off my things. I found Bradley standing at the front door.

"Hi, honey, I'm home," I say with a little laugh.

"Hey, gorgeous, welcome home," Bradley pulls me into his arms and gives me a long, lingering kiss. "Shall we crack open the Champagne now or later?"

"Let's have it now, then we can decide where to put all my stuff."

"Okay, I got the guys to put it all in the spare room for now so you can go through it at your own pace. After all, you have taken a week off work to move," he says with a smirk.

"It will take me all that time to get it sorted, trust me."

"Come on." He grabs my hand and pulls me into the house. I kick the front door closed as he leads me into the kitchen, a bottle of my favourite pink Champagne sitting in an ice bucket on the table.

Bradley opens the bottle with a loud bang as the cork pops, he pours two glasses and hands me one.

"Here's to your new home and our life together."

We clink our glasses together and I gulp mine, emptying the glass. Bradley swiftly refills my glass.

"I have booked a table at The Crypt restaurant tonight to celebrate and save us cooking."

"That's lovely, we will cook at some point though, mister. It's nice to eat out and have takeaways, but not all the time."

"Okay, you can help me learn to cook," he says and gives me a kiss.

"I will."

We finish our glasses of Champagne then head upstairs to the spare room. I look at the pile and try to decide which box to start with. Bradley slides his hands around my waist and pulls me back against him. I can feel his hard cock as it presses against me. His tongue licks the side of my neck and he traces kisses around the back of my neck. My body relaxes into his as he slowly grinds his cock against my arse.

"Bradley, I have work to do," I say in a poor attempt to stop him.

"That stuff isn't going anywhere," he whispers, his breath warming my ear as he nibbles my lobe. I can feel my cock stiffening as his hands slide over my belly and up to my chest as he starts unbuttoning my shirt.

I can't resist him as he undoes the last button and his hands touch my smooth belly. He moans heavily in my ear. Moving his hands up to my chest, he brushes over my stiff nipples, making me moan with pleasure. He takes my nipples between his thumbs and index fingers, twisting them hard as he squeezes them tight. I call out in a blissful mixture of pleasure and pain.

"You enjoy that, don't you, gorgeous?" he says with a breathy tone.

"Yes, sir."

He continues squeezing and teasing my nipples as he grinds his hard cock against me.

"Drop your trousers and pants," he demands.

I undo my trousers and they drop to my feet. The front of my boxers wet with pre-cum, I ease them off, freeing my hard cock.

Letting go of my right nipple, he shifts his hand to my cock, rubbing his palm over the wet head before gripping tightly around the shaft. He gently bites the back of my neck as he slides his hand up and down my cock, pulling my foreskin back harder each time. Bradley knows all the little things that easily take me to the edge. I'm pushing back and grinding against his cock as his hand rubs faster.

"Bradley, I'm going to come soon," I say between heavy breaths.

"Not yet," he growls. Letting go of my cock, I hear him undo his belt and unzip his jeans. His cock, also wet with pre-cum, pushes between my arse cheeks, sliding into my hole with ease. He shifts me closer to the wall and I place my hands against it as he thrusts in and out of me. Pre-cum drips from my cock with every push into me. He grips my cock again, pulling the skin back hard as he fucks me, I can feel my balls tightening, ready to shoot.

"I can't hold back any longer," I call out as cum shoots, hitting my belly and the floor, losing control as my body spasms. My legs shake as he rams his cock fast and hard into me. A few harder fucks and he roars out as his cum shoots deep inside me. He pulls me tight against him and grinds his cock in me, shooting the last of his load. Holding onto me to steady himself, his breathing is heavy in my ear. He hugs me tight for a while before pulling his cock out of me. Turning me to face him, he gives me a lingering kiss, our wet, softening cocks crushed between our bodies.

"Welcome home, sweetheart," he says.

"Good to be here, handsome."

"We best get cleaned up before putting these things away."

"Yeah, I am a sticky mess thanks to you," I say with a laugh.

"I didn't hear you complaining about it."

"No chance; the more the merrier."

"Get in that bathroom," he says smacking my arse.

We both get cleaned up and dressed before unpacking two boxes. Time flew by and before we knew it we had to get ready to go to The Crypt. We hurriedly shower together to save time, although I could spend hours in a shower with Bradley lathering up my body, but we will have plenty of time for that now that I'm living here.

Once we're ready, we head out to the restaurant. This place will always be special as it is where we went on the night we first met.

The man on reception shows us down the stairs to

the restaurant. As he opens the door at the bottom of the stairs I hear the cello and piano playing. A warm feeling flows through me, as though I have just come home from a long trip, making my skin tingle as the man shows us to our table. If I'm not mistaken, this is the same table we dined at that first night.

"I love this place; I get lost in the music," I say, smiling at Bradley.

"Yes, it has very fond memories."

The waiter comes over and hands us the menus. Before I can speak, Bradley orders a bottle of pink Champagne, we place our food orders and he whisks himself away from the table.

"I never would have thought that night we met that we would be here all these months later, having moved in together."

"Well, I hope you have got over your fears of living together."

I laugh at his comment. "Mandy has told me off enough times, so, yes, I'm over the fears."

"Good, why don't you invite Mandy to dinner one night? I would love to meet her."

"She would love that, I will send her a message tomorrow."

The waiter returns with the Champagne and pours a small amount for me to taste. I try my best to look like I know what I'm tasting it for. Giving it a quick swirl in the glass and smelling it before sipping it, then nodding at the waiter. Bradley gives me a cheeky smile, he knows I know nothing about wine and finds it funny when I put on a show. The waiter pours our glasses and puts the bottle into an ice bucket on a stand at the side of the table.

"So, what could you smell? Apples, maybe some white flowers?" he says with a little laugh.

"Don't wind me up," I snap at him.

"I'm only playing, sweetheart." He picks up his glass. "Here's to us and our future together." Holding his glass, waiting for me to raise mine, he entwines the fingers of his other hand with mine.

I raise my glass and clink it against his, giving him a smile and a little giggle.

We chat away whilst we wait for the food to arrive; our conversation stops while we eat the meal. The food is a wonderful as I remember. After another bottle and dessert, we head back home. Walking along, I hold on to Bradley's arm as I feel a little lightheaded from the drink. I'm sure he tops up my glass more than his own as he does not seem at all drunk.

By the time we get home, it is late, so we head off to bed, my first night snuggling up to Bradley in my new home. I drift off into a peaceful contented sleep.

23

I'm woken by Bradley hugging me I can feel his hard cock nestled against my arse and his strong arms holding me tight. I smile to myself as I snuggle back into him.

"Morning, sweetheart," he whispers in my ear.

"Morning," I grab his arm and hold it tighter to my chest enjoying him being so close.

He pushes his cock against my arse cheeks. "I love waking up with you in my arms," he says in a low sexy voice.

"I love it too." I slowly rub my arse back against his cock; we are both morning sex guys. Well, to be honest, where Bradley's concerned I'm an anytime he wants it guy.

He shifts on the bed and I feel his hand adjust his cock, pushing it between my cheeks and pressing against the head into my hole. I moan with appreciation as he grinds himself deeper into me. He slides his hand down

185

my belly, reaching for my stiff cock. Gripping it, he pulls the skin back and runs his finger over the slit, rubbing the pre-cum over the head as he continues his slow thrusts in and out of me.

"Oh, yes, that feels good," I mumble as his fist grips tighter and strokes my cock faster.

His thrusts into me getting faster and deeper as his breath becomes heavy. I wrap my leg over his, allowing him to get deeper into me. He responds by pushing his cock harder and deeper. I can feel his pubic hair as he grinds against my arse.

My balls tighten as his fist squeezes and rams my skin back hard. I call out from the pain of my skin stretching as it makes me cum. Still gripping my shaft, he slams his cock in and out of me, then roars as he shoots inside me. Collapsing against my back, he breathes heavy, his breath warming my skin.

"That felt great," I say as I turn to face him.

"I hope I didn't hurt you?"

"No, it felt great, you know I love having my skin stretched back hard."

"That's okay then." He kisses me softly, his tongue tracing along my lips. "Morning again, gorgeous."

"Morning, handsome, I love you so much."

"As I do you."

He pulls me into his arms, wrapping his legs around mine as he kisses me deeply.

We cuddle together in the bed for a while, enjoying the closeness of each other. Shifting on the bed, I lay with my head on his chest, listening to his heart thudding deep inside. I could spend hours lying like this, lost in our own world.

After half an hour, Bradley suggests we get up shower and have breakfast before continuing the chore of unpacking my things. I reluctantly agree as I would rather lay in bed together all day.

Having got showered and dressed we head down to the kitchen and Bradley prepares bacon, eggs, and toast.

I sit at the table and laugh to myself as I watch him trying to juggle everything to get it cooked at the same time. He finally puts the food on the table and sits down.

"Dig in," he says giving me a smile.

"It looks lovely, thank you."

"Make the most of it; you're cooking next Sunday."

"It will be my pleasure," I reply, winking at him.

"Okay, I have a confession to make."

I almost choke on my toast as the words left his mouth. "What confession?" I ask, my heart beating faster. I'm unsure what he is about to say.

"I have a housekeeper."

"That doesn't surprise me, I didn't imagine you cleaning this house," I laugh, relieved that was all he had to confess.

"His name is Sebastian, he has worked for me for two years now."

"Sebastian!" I'm sure he heard the change in the tone of my voice. "So, it's a *male* housekeeper."

"Yes, I'm sure you will like him. He will be here tomorrow, he works from one to six."

"He's here every day?" I say with surprise.

"Monday to Friday, that's why you have never met him before." He can sense I'm not that happy about this news. "You will like him, I promise, he won't get in your way."

"Okay, I will get to meet him tomorrow then."

"Yes, he knows you will be here, and he is looking forward to meeting you."

I carry on eating my breakfast whilst pondering in my head how I feel about having a housekeeper now that I am living here. Bradley stays quiet letting me think, he knows how to handle me, he seems to have learned a lot about me in the time we have been together.

We finish our breakfast and I help Bradley load the dishwasher. As I bend down, he squeezes my arse. "You going to give me a smile then?" he asks.

I stand up and smile at him. "How could I not smile for you, my lovely man."

He pulls me into his arms and kisses me. "Good, I want to keep you smiling. Let's have a look at where we can fit your things."

"Okay."

We head upstairs and Bradley shows me the space he has made for me in the wardrobe for my clothes. There are also some empty drawers. Then he opens a door next to his bedroom door revealing a small stair-case that leads up to the loft. I follow him up the stairs, someone has converted the loft into another huge room. All that is up there is a few storage boxes, an arm chair, an old chest of drawers, and wardrobe.

"You can store anything up here," he says.

"Well, you are not lacking space, that's for sure."

"Not at all!"

We spend the rest of the day putting things away and I have to stop Bradley from laughing at some of my old clothes. He enjoys winding me up at times, but it is something I find endearing about him. The day seems to fly by, we had a takeaway for dinner, then headed to bed early as Bradley has an early start because he's flying to the US for a few meetings.

I've spent the morning unpacking boxes and finding places to store my things. Keeping an eye on the clock as I await Sebastian's arrival. I'm curious to see what he is like and to find out something about him. After all, he has been in Bradley's life longer than me. As I hang shirts onto hangers, I hear the front door close.

"*Hola*," he called out, the Spanish accent heavy in his voice.

I walk to the top of the stairs and look down at him. He is about five-feet-eight, shoulder length straight black hair, dark tanned skin. He looks as fit as fuck. A white linen shirt is attached to his body like a second skin, unbuttoned to below the centre of his hairless chest. He has skimpy jean shorts that seem to reveal more than I feel comfortable with, knowing he has been around Bradley dressed like that.

"Hey," I say, grabbing his attention. He looks up the stairs.

"*Hola*, I'm Sebastian, you are David," his voice is as hot as his body.

"Hi, Bradley told me you would be here today." I walk down the stairs feeling rather under-dressed in my joggers and a sweatshirt. I hold out my hand to shake his. His fingers brush against mine as he lightly grips my hand. "Good to meet you."

"Yes, you too, Bradley has mentioned much about you."

I'm a little taken back that Bradley is talking about me to his housekeeper. As he walks into the kitchen I follow him.

"Can I get you a drink?" he asks, as though it is his house.

"I would love a coffee." I try to ignore his familiarity and sit down at the table, watching him as he floats around the kitchen, filling the kettle and grabbing the cups.

"So, have you known Bradley long?" I ask.

"About three years. I met him at The Crypt, I clean there in the mornings.

"Oh, yeah, we have been there a few times."

"Yes, he is there a lot." He leans against the counter waiting for the kettle to boil, one hand on his hip as he bites the little finger on his other hand. I can see his eyes flickering as he looks me up and down. For the first time in a long time I feel a little insecure about my body as I wonder what he is thinking about me

The kettle whistles, breaking the awkward silence, and he turns away. He makes the coffee and hands me a cup.

"So, what is your cleaning routine?" I ask.

"I usually put the washing in the machine, whilst I clean around the rooms downstairs, then I go upstairs, finishing with ironing anything that is clean and dry."

"Okay, I'm upstairs finding homes for my things." I leave the kitchen uneasy about the way he looked at me. I know I'm not a fit, hot guy, but Bradley loves me as I am.

We stay out of each other's way for most of the afternoon. Although I feel relieved when he calls out to say he's heading home. My first impression is that I don't like him, but then I won't see him once I go back to work.

I settle in the lounge after eating a pizza for dinner, my phone beside me as I wait for Bradley to call. I'm pondering what to say about Sebastian when the phone rings.

"Hello."

"Hi, gorgeous, how's things over there? Are you settling in okay?"

I love hearing his voice when he is away, he always seems so pleased to be talking to me.

"Hey, handsome, yeah I'm getting sorted. Missing you though, the bed will be empty without you snuggling up tonight."

"I'm missing you too, but it will be nice when I get back."

"How are the meetings going?"

"All good so far, thanks, talking of meetings, what do you think of Sebastian?" He must have heard the deep breath I took, "Come on, tell me the truth."

"I'm not sure about him, we didn't click, and he looks at me funny."

Bradley laughed. "He is only there to keep the place tidy, I didn't expect you to be best friends. What do you mean he looks at you funny?"

"He made me feel conscious about my weight."

"That's not like you to worry about things like that. I love you as you are, so don't worry about what he thinks. You're my Chuddly."

"Chuddly, what kind of word is that?" I ask with a laugh.

"Chubby and cuddly, Chuddly and I wouldn't have you any other way."

He always lifts my spirits. "I will have to think of a word for you."

"As long as it's nice, but, seriously, don't get wound up by Sebastian, most of the time you won't even see him."

"Okay, I will try to ignore him."

"Good, unfortunately, this will have to be a short one tonight as I have more meetings to go to. I will make sure I have longer to chat tomorrow."

"Well, don't work too hard. I can't wait for you to get back."

"I can't wait either. Sweet dreams, Chuddly."

"Sweet dreams, love you loads."

"Love you too, night-night."

"Night."

The phone clicks in my ear and I hear a dial tone.

I wish I could be with him everywhere he goes; now

that I have him, I don't want to be without him. I decide to have an early night and cuddle up to his pillow in bed, drifting off to a peaceful sleep, a blissfully warm glow inside. I've never been this happy in my life.

24

S till home alone, I have a look in the loft to see if I can find any old pictures of Bradley before Sebastian arrives. There is a chest of drawers to one side. I open the top drawer and discover it has about twenty-five small boxes. Lifting one out, I open it to find a very nice gold watch with a black leather strap inside. Placing it back, I open another box to find a silver metal watch. Opening a few more boxes they all have different styles of watches in them. It must be another one of Bradley's fetishes, I laugh to myself.

I close the drawer and open the next one down. This drawer is full of T-shirts all neatly folded. Opening the last drawer, it has old ties, belts, and boxes of cufflinks. I push the drawer shut and walk over to the wardrobe. Suits covered in plastic hang from the rail, then I see two storage boxes on the shelf below. I pick up one box and carry it over to the chest of drawers, placing on top.

Lifting the lid, I sigh, at last, the box is full of photo albums. I take the first album and sit on the old arm chair. The first page has photos of children playing in a garden, I recognise Albert and Lucy although they are a few years younger. Turning the pages there are several more photos of Bradley's sister's children. Then I find a photo with Bradley sitting at a table, another guy next to him with his arm over Bradley's shoulder. I take a sharp breath, I wanted to find some of his past photos, but I never thought about seeing photos of him with his ex-partners. That didn't enter my mind.

I lift the album closer to my face so I can check out the guy. He looks nothing like me; blond hair, well-toned body. I try not to dwell on the photo too much, but my curiosity makes me stare. I continue turning the pages. It's not long before I come across another one, this time a closer shot of their faces, with the other guy kissing Bradley's cheek. Twinges of jealously hit me as I look at the photo, why I do not understand. He is bound to have had past relationships. Closing the album, I walk back to the box, my curiosity getting the better of me. Picking up another album, I flick through the pages. These look like holiday photos from some exotic location, including more of the blond-haired guy in various poses. I can't see what he saw in him myself, but then Bradley would probably think that about Craig if he saw a photo of him.

Bored with this album I get one more out of the box, I'm looking for photos of a younger Bradley. A white, shimmery album at the bottom of the box catches my eye. I pull it out and sit back on the chair. The album has the words wedding written in silver across the front. This must be photos from Helen and Stuart's wedding. I open the album and the first photo is of a younger Bradley holding hands with a bride. His smile as gorgeous as ever. This is what I was looking for. He was stunning when he was younger, not that he isn't now. But then I realise it's not Helen in the photo. It can't be Helen's wedding then, it must be one of his friends. I turn the page, the next photo is another with him and the bride this time they are closer and he is kissing her on the lips, the people nearby throwing confetti over them.

My hands sweat and shake as the reality of what I'm seeing in the photos hits me. This isn't someone else's wedding, this is Bradley's wedding. My heartbeat quickens as I frantically turn the pages. Photo after photo of him and this woman. I lift my hand to cover my mouth and my blood runs cold. I can't believe what I'm seeing. He was married to a woman.

Tears fill my eyes as my hands shake, my breathing erratic. He has never mentioned this. I know I wanted to know more about his past, but this isn't what I was expecting to find. My body trembles as the images of them kissing etch into my mind. Looking around the loft, I can't move, I'm frozen to the spot by the shock. Why has he never mentioned he was married before? Does he still see his wife? My world is crashing around me and I don't know what to do.

The front door slams. Sebastian calling out brings me back to the moment. I quickly throw the album back in the box and put it away in the wardrobe. Wiping my eyes, I try to compose myself before heading downstairs.

Sebastian is already in the kitchen, boiling the kettle, when I get there.

"Morning, are you okay?" he asks, noticing my red eyes and flushed complexion.

"Yeah, I'm okay, I just had a little shocking news, that's all."

"Do you want to talk about it, I'm a good listener," he replies as he pours water into the cups.

"Thanks for the offer, but I'm still trying to work it out in my head."

He hands me the coffee. "Well, I'm here if you want to chat."

"Thanks, I'm going to go and lie down in the bedroom for a while."

"Okay, I will try not to be too noisy."

I head back up to the bedroom and shut the door. Putting my coffee on the side, I pick up my phone and call Mandy.

"Hey, I was thinking about you this morning, how's the holiday going? Are you settling into the house?" she asks.

Hearing her voice overwhelms me and my emotions take over as I burst into tears down the phone.

"David, what's wrong?" Her tone becomes more serious with concern.

"Oh, Mandy, I've just found out Bradley was married," I struggle to say between tears and gasps for breath.

"What? How did you find that out?"

"I was looking through his old photo albums and

found one with wedding photos," I struggle to say. "He was married to a woman. I don't know what to do,"

"Oh my God, does Bradley know you were looking at the albums?"

"No, I was curious about his past and found them whilst I was putting things away in the loft."

"David, what did you do that for? You and your curiosity always get you into trouble," her motherly tone now kicking into the conversation.

"I was just looking for photos of him when he was younger," I reply in a low, whimpering voice.

"You could have just asked him to show you photos. You didn't have to go snooping around looking for them." Her telling me off for snooping pulls me back into reality, Mandy always has a way of looking at things sensibly. "When was this wedding?"

"I don't know, there are no dates in the album."

"So, you're getting yourself all upset about something he hasn't mentioned that may have been many years ago. He is obviously divorced or he wouldn't be planning to marry you."

"I suppose you're right, but I thought our wedding was the first time for us both."

"I can understand that upsetting you, but everyone has a history, David. Perhaps he hasn't told you to protect you. You don't know his reasons, the problem you have now is how do you bring it up with Bradley to find out the whole truth?"

I've stopped crying and my thoughts now turn to the point she has raised.

"I hadn't thought about that. What is he going to

think about me?" My upset now turns to worry about his reaction.

"Knowing you, he will realise something is wrong as soon as he gets back, let's face it, you're not great about hiding your emotions."

"You're right, as always."

"You need to stop worrying about it and have a conversation with Bradley when he gets home. I'm sure there is a good reason he hasn't mentioned it before. But don't let something from his past stop you two from having a future."

"Okay, I will try to forget about it until he gets back I promise," My head is in a muddle as I try to make sense of everything.

"I've got to go back to work, if I don't hear from you before, I will see you Friday evening."

"Okay, thanks, Mandy. Yes, I'm looking forward to dinner and you meeting Bradley. Don't work too hard."

"It's manic here without you, make the most of your break and let me know how you get on with him."

"I will do, thanks again, sorry for the drama." I try to sound more in control of my emotions.

"Your life is full of drama that's why I love you. Chat later," she says laughing as she hangs up the phone.

Sitting down on the bed, I drink my coffee, pondering what Mandy has said before lying down for a little nap. I must have fallen asleep as I'm woken by Sebastian calling out to see if I want another coffee. Heading back downstairs I sit in the kitchen with him and listen to him telling me all about what happened when he was out the night before. Most of what he says is going in one ear and out the other as my mind is to wrapped up in Bradley's wedding.

I decide to go out for a walk to clear my head. By the time I get back, Sebastian has gone home. I cook myself a Bolognese, then sit on the sofa, waiting for Bradley to call. Turning on the sound system blasts eighties music into the room. I would normally dance around the room, but I'm not in the mood this evening. I need to make sure he doesn't realise there is anything wrong whilst he is on the phone.

After about an hour, his face appears on my phone as it rings next to me.

"Hello, handsome, how are you doing?" I say, keeping my voice upbeat.

"Hey, gorgeous, all is well, missing you lots. I wish you could come on these trips with me."

"So do I, the place feels lonely without you here."

"Well, I'm back home tomorrow and horny as hell for you. What have you been up to today?"

I laugh at his comment. "Not as horny as I am. I finished putting the last of my things away, I had a chat with Mandy on the phone and went for a walk by the river this afternoon."

"How is Mandy? I bet she is missing you as well?"

"Yeah, she said it has been busy at work. I'm not looking forward to going back."

"That's because you have had a break from it, once you're there I'm sure it will be okay."

"You're probably right. How has your day been?"

"Just endless meetings, I'm trying to get as much

done as I can so I don't have to come over here as often. Then I can spend more time with you."

"Aww, you're so lovely, you always say the sweetest things."

"You've made me realise work's not everything."

"Wow, I never thought I would hear you say that."

"I never thought I would say it, but you, my Chuddly, are my world now."

I bite my lip and my heart beats faster as I remember the photos in the album. Worrying about how he will feel when he finds out I went snooping.

"As you are mine," I say still trying to hide my emotions.

"Well, I best get on with these meetings so I can get back to you."

"Okay, don't work to hard, I love you."

"Love you too, see you tomorrow."

The phone cuts off and I stare around the room. My mind is a mess as I go over the events of the day.

25

I'm sitting on the sofa when Bradley opens the front door.

"Hey, Chuddly, I'm home," he calls out as he closes the door.

Jumping up from the sofa I run into the hallway and he pulls me into his arms. Hugging me tight against him, his lips press to mine. The warmth of his body makes me relax. His kiss lingers as he hugs me tighter. I can tell he has missed me as much as I have missed him.

Breaking away from the kiss, he looks into my eyes. "This is how I want it to be whenever I come home," he says before kissing me again.

"I've missed you so much," I say between kisses.

His tongue pushes into my mouth and I feel his hard cock grind against me. "I'm back now and I want you," he whispers.

"Downstairs or upstairs?" I ask.

"Upstairs. I want to enjoy every inch of you."

Leaving his case in the hall, he takes my hand and leads me upstairs.

Entering the bedroom, he pulls me back close to him, his mouth inches from mine, the warmth of his breath heating my lips. Desire glowing in his eyes as he stares into mine, my cock stiffens. His lips press softly against mine as I close my eyes. The smell of his cologne lingers, heightening my senses as his tongue pushes deep into my mouth. He crushes me to the wall and grinds himself against me as our tongues entwine passionately.

Stepping away from me, he pulls my sweatshirt off over my head, his hands returning to my sides. He kisses the side of my neck. Moving up to my ear, he sucks my lobe between his lips and nibbles lightly, sending shivers down my spine. My nipples stiffening from his touch and the chill of the room. He slides his hand over my belly and up to my nipple. He kisses along the underside of my chin as he squeezes and twists my nipple. Pain shoots across my chest and my cock throbs, leaking into my pants.

"Turn around," he demands in a low growl.

He softly kisses the back of my neck, his tongue tracing wet trails between each kiss as he works his way down the centre of my back, stopping at the base of my spine. He pulls my joggers to the floor, revealing my tight white pants. I hear him moan with approval as he traces his tongue across my back above the waistline. His hands slide up the inside of my legs. My eyes are closed as I lose myself in his touch.

His hands slide from between my legs, brushing over my arse before grabbing the waistband of my pants, pulling them down to my feet. My cock hits my belly, wet and sticky with pre-cum. I feel his face push into my arse as his tongue searches out my hole. His hands pull my cheeks apart and he teases the soft outer skin of my hole, licking and pushing his tongue into my arse. My moans of pleasure echo loudly around the room as I push back against his face. My balls tighten against my body as pre-cum drips from my cock. I grab my cock and rub it hard in my fist pulling the foreskin back tight with each stroke.

His tongue stretches my hole as it pushes inside, making me wet and ready for his cock to follow. I pant heavily as his tongue traces up my spine. Standing, I hear him unzip his trousers before feeling his cock push between my cheeks. Sliding his hands around my belly, he pulls me back against him as he pushes his cock deep into me. Growling into my ear, he presses his cock deeper before pulling back out of me and ramming it back in hard. He fucks me hard and fast as I press one of my hands to the wall to steady myself. "Oh, yes, fuck me hard," I shout as I push back against his cock. My hand vigorously stroking my cock, I roar as cum shoots from my throbbing dick.

Hearing me cum he bites the back of my neck, squeezing my belly tighter as he pushes his cock as deep into me as he can. Thrusting faster and faster, his breathing gets heavy and I can tell he is about to come. I move one hand to his arse, pulling him harder against me. He lets out a loud growl. I feel his cock throbbing, his cum shooting deep inside me. His hands grab onto me to steady himself as his orgasm makes his legs shake.

Holding his cock deep inside me, he kisses my neck gently before pulling himself out of me. I turn and face him as we both smile at each other. "Welcome home, handsome," I say between breaths.

"That was a wonderful welcome home. I love you," he says, then kisses me. "Let's have a quick shower and then get something to eat."

"Sounds good to me."

Once we have showered and dressed, we order a pizza for dinner and Bradley tells me more about his trip whilst we eat and have a few glasses on wine. After we have eaten, we head to the lounge and sit on the sofa.

I can't hold back any longer. "I found some photos in the loft," I blurt out.

"What photos?" He stares at me, calm and relaxed.

"A wedding album." My eyes well up as my hands shake, unsure what his reply will be.

"Oh, I see." His voice is a low, calm tone as he looks deep into my eyes. "Yes, I was married twenty years ago."

"How come you never mentioned it?" I snap at him.

"Because it's history, I was only married for six months. It never worked out, and we divorced soon after. There isn't much to tell you."

"Are you still in touch with her?"

"No, I haven't seen her since we split, what does it matter anyway? We're not together anymore." The calmness in his voice is gone.

"I think it's something you should have mentioned."

"Why? How does something that happened twenty years ago, before I even knew you, affect us?"

"I thought our wedding would be the first time and special for both of us. I was shocked and upset to find the photos," I say, the words coming out before I can think.

He shakes his head at the comment. "How did you find the photos anyway? They're in a storage box in the wardrobe in the loft?" His voice changes, I can tell he is getting angry with me now.

"Looking for some old photos to see what you looked like when you were younger," I mumble, knowing I was in the wrong and feeling guilty about what I had done.

"So, you went prying around in my things," he snaps. "You could have just asked me to show you some photos. I have nothing to hide from you, David."

"I know. I'm sorry, but I wasn't expecting to find wedding photos and it upset me to find out you've already been married." I wipe the tears from my face.

Realising what had really upset me, he pulls me into him, "Come here." My head nestles into his neck and my tears wet his skin.

"The marriage was more about what people expected me to do at the time. I was only eighteen and back then coming out as gay wasn't the done thing. I knew it wasn't right, and that's why it never lasted long. She avoided me after we split and I haven't heard from her since. I want to marry you and I want everyone to see us get married. Because I love you more than anything in the world and our wedding will be very special."

The overwhelming relief flows through me as I hear

those words. "I'm sorry I went snooping, I love you so much."

"I love you, more than you realise, and I'm sorry if it upset you. I should have told you but, honestly, it was so long ago." He gives me a kiss. "Come on, Chuddly, the past is over; let's make our wedding a day to remember."

"I want it to be an amazing day."

"It will be, trust me, because you mean the world to me."

"I trust you." I kiss him, then hug him.

"Come on, it's been a long day, let's get to sleep."

26

"What time is she due to arrive?" Bradley asks as he checks the wine in the fridge.

"About seven. Don't worry, everything will be ready."

"I still think we should have gotten Richard from The Crypt to do the cooking."

"Mandy will be fine with what I'm cooking, I have cooked for her loads of times at my flat," I reply, a hint of annoyance in my voice.

"Okay, sorry, I'm a little nervous about meeting her."

"I've never seen you so nervous. Why? It's only Mandy?"

"But I feel like I'm meeting your Mum, the way you talk about her."

"Don't be silly, she will love you." I give him a kiss and then check the meat in the oven.

"I hope so," he says, still pacing around the kitchen.

"Okay, let's get ready, everything is fine down here."

Bradley pulls me into his body. "I love you, Chud-dly," he says before kissing me.

"I love you too, now let's get changed before she arrives."

We have just finished getting ready when the door-bell rings. Rushing downstairs, I open the door.

"Hey, Mandy, come on in." I gesture her into the house. "This is Bradley."

"Hi, it's nice to meet you after all this one has told me about you," Mandy says.

Bradley gives her a kiss on each cheek and says, "Likewise, it's lovely to meet you." She smiles.

I give her a big hug. "Let me take your jacket."

"Would you like a drink?" Bradley asks.

"I would love a glass of wine, please."

"Red or white?"

"Oh, white, too much red gives me a headache."

"Come through," Bradley leads her into the lounge, "have a seat."

Eighties music is playing in the background, I can see Mandy checking out the room, her smile telling me she approves.

"I will get the drinks," Bradley says.

"So, what do you think?" I whisper to her once he has left the room.

"He is lovely, I wouldn't mind him myself."

"Hands off, he's already taken." I laugh.

"Is everything okay now after the photo album incident?"

"Yeah, it's all sorted."

"Great, this place is wonderful."

"It's fantastic! I love the place and Bradley."

"Did I hear my name?" he asks as he walks back in the room carrying a tray of drinks.

"I was telling Mandy how much I love you."

"That's okay then." He hands Mandy a glass, then gives me mine before sitting on the opposite sofa.

Mandy and I chat about work and Bradley sits, listening. I can see him smirk now and then as he hears about the staff antics at work. I head to the kitchen to finish dinner, leaving them two to chat. Once it is ready, I call them into the dining room. Mandy looks even more impressed by this room as she sits at the large dining table. I serve the starters, halloumi on a bed of salad, drizzled with a balsamic glaze, and Bradley pours more wine.

"This looks nice," she says.

"Thanks, I did the cooking, as it's not one of Bradley's best qualities."

"Yes, I have to admit that, but I cook a mean breakfast," he says with a laugh.

We all finish the starter then I bring in the main course, lamb with vegetables. Conversation is slow as we eat the meal, but they are obviously enjoying the food. We finish with a lemon panna cotta. They both congratulate me on the food. Bradley offers to clear the table while we go back to the lounge with another glass of wine.

Mandy comments that there is no TV in the room, so I show her how the TV comes out from the wall. She is impressed by all the technology in the house. We talk about work for a little while until Bradley comes back into the room holding another bottle of wine.

"More wine anyone?"

"Well it would be rude not to accept," she says.

"I will have to get you to tell me all David's secrets one day," he says as he fills her glass.

"I'm sure you already know most of them."

"Very true," he replies.

"So, how are the wedding plans coming along? Have you set a date yet for the big day?"

"I have been so busy sorting things to move in, we haven't had time to arrange anything yet."

"Well, whenever it is, I will make sure I'm there."

"You better be there, I was hoping you would give me away," I say.

Mandy blushes. "Oh, I would love that. Definitely."

"Yay, that's one thing settled then. I have my best woman."

"That's great," Bradley says. "I may regret this but I'm going to give David free range to organise the day he wants. All I want is to pick the music for the ceremony and the first dance," he says with a smile at me.

"Aww, that's a deal." A huge smile spreads across my face.

"You might want to set him a budget and keep an eye on what he's planning," she says.

"I will trust you to do that, I'm sure you will keep his feet firmly on the ground. But I want it to be a special day he never forgets."

"It will be a lovely day, I'm sure."

"Yes, I can arrive in a pink carriage with white

horses, dressed in a pink suit." I say, trying to keep a serious face.

"Remember, it's a wedding, not a circus show," Bradley says the tone of his voice very serious.

I laugh. "I'm joking! It will be a traditional affair, with just a little hint of David, I promise."

"Well, Mandy will make sure of that as your best woman."

"I will indeed," she says.

We spend the rest of the evening chatting and drinking. Bradley kept trying to get Mandy to tell him things about me but she wouldn't say anything. It was really nice having her over for the evening and helped to make me feel at home. Mandy left about ten thirty, then we went to bed, snuggling up together and drifting off into a deep sleep.

27

I'm woken by Bradley nestling behind me, his cock hard and pushing between my arse cheeks. It's always the best wake up call. I snuggle back against him, my sweaty arse and his pre-cum let his cock slide into me with ease. His moans of pleasure sync with mine as I feel his pubic hair brush against my arse, his cock throbbing deep inside me. He gently rocks behind me, grinding himself as deep as he can, then as he kisses the back of my neck. His hairy chest rubs against my smooth skin, sending prickles across my back. Pulling the covers off us, I relax and push back onto him. The physical connection always takes our feelings for each other to another level. His right hand slides around my belly and down towards my dick. Gripping my hard cock, he slowly strokes my foreskin back using my pre-cum to lubricate his hand and my shaft.

I push my cock into his fist as he twists it around my shaft, dragging my skin back, making me grind my arse back onto his cock as he strokes mine faster and faster. The pleasure I'm feeling of his cock rubbing over my prostate makes my cock leak more. The attention he is giving both my dick and arse is heaven. It's not long before I'm bucking and growling like a wild animal as he pounds my arse and yanks my foreskin back, pushing me over the edge. I roar as cum shoots onto the bed. I'm panting for breath, his cock still deep inside me. Even though I'm desperate for him to fuck me hard, I pull his cock out of me as I shift on the bed and push him onto his back. I straddle his stomach and entwine my fingers into his chest hair. Pressing my lips to his, I kiss him deeply, my tongue exploring his mouth as his hands pull my arse cheeks apart. The cool air excites my gaping, wet hole.

Sitting up on my knees, I grab his hard dick, rubbing the head over my hole. I'm not sure who I'm teasing the most, but I want to feel him deep inside me again as I sit back onto his throbbing cock. We both moan loudly, his full length sliding into my arse as I settle onto his balls. I watch the pleasure in his face as I sit still, feeling him throbbing inside. Running my fingers through his chest hair, I squeeze his nipples, his expression giving away the pleasure he is experiencing with each twist.

Slowly, I rock back and forth on his cock, grinding him against my prostate. My softening cock still leaks onto his stomach. Smiling at me as I lift my arse up and down on his cock, his fingers reach my nipples and squeeze them hard before twisting and pulling them. The pain shooting across my chest makes me slam down and growl at him.

"Turn around," he demands.

Keeping him deep inside, I twist around, lifting my leg over him and place my hands on his knees. Now facing away from him, he pushes on my arse to lift it off his dick, leaving just the head inside.

"That looks good," he says as he moves in and out of me. I can tell the sight of his cock sliding into my hole is turning him on more as his thrusts get faster. I can hear his breathing get louder as he rapidly pounds my hole. Pulling me down onto his cock until it's deep inside, he roars, filling me with warm cum. I slowly grind on him until he slaps my arse giving me a sign to stop.

I lift myself off him, his warm cum leaking out of me as I lie down next to him. He wraps his arm around me and pulls me against his body, my head resting on his chest. I slide my leg between his and gently play with his chest hair.

"That was a nice wake up call," I say.

"It's not time to get up yet, let's have a few more minutes."

"Okay." I'm not going to argue with him; the opportunity to lay and cuddle together in bed is not to be missed.

His breathing slows as he falls back to sleep, I snuggle closer to him, the warmth of his body making me glow inside as I drift off to sleep.

I'm woken by the letter box banging as the postman shoves the mail through the door.

"What time is it?" Bradley asks.

"Nine thirty."

"We better get up. I'm supposed to be working from home today."

I give him a lingering kiss. "But this is nicer than work."

"Yes, it is, but it won't pay the bills. Come on, I need a shower." He slaps my arse as he gets off the bed.

"Oh, yes, more; please." I laugh.

"Careful what you wish for, Chuddly."

"You can spank me anytime."

"I'm still holding you to that from your last offer."

I watch him walk slowly around the bed towards the bathroom, his cock semi-hard and looking very tasty. I could happily spend the day naked in bed with him. He is so handsome, I still can't believe we are together.

Hearing the shower start, I roll onto my back, staring up at the ceiling. My thoughts turn to the wedding and what I would like on the day. Do I want a big lavish affair or a quiet, little ceremony?

Bradley walks back into the room, distracting me from my thoughts, the white towel over his shoulder making his tan look even darker. Droplets of water glisten as they hang from the hair on his chest. My cock stirs as I admire his athletic body. As I get off the bed, I glimpse myself in the mirror my skin pale and smooth. My chubby belly wobbles as I walk past Bradley. He grabs my arm and embraces me against his skin, cool and wet. His mouth presses to mine and his tongue slides between my lips. Grabbing my arse his kiss is long and lingering.

"I love you, Chuddly."

"I love you too."

"Good, now go and shower." He squeezes my arse and gives me another quick kiss. "I will rustle up some breakfast."

"Okay."

After showering I get dressed and head downstairs. Bradley is cooking a bacon and cheese omelette.

"Something smells nice."

"A special omelette for my special man. Grab a seat, it's almost ready."

I sit at the table and take a sip of my coffee. Putting the plates on the table, he sits opposite me.

"So, what date do you think we should go with for the wedding?" Bradley asks.

"Sometime in November? I like the autumn."

"What about the weather? it could pour with rain?"

"The rain would only affect the photos, we could have them taken inside if we need to," I say.

"Okay, where would you like to get married?" Bradley asks.

"I've always dreamed of marrying in a big posh stately home, something like the house in the TV programme *Downton Abbey*. Then we can have the wedding and reception in the same place."

"I'm sure we could find somewhere like that. Do you want to arrange the wedding with Mandy or would you prefer a wedding planner to help?"

"What about your input to the wedding?" I ask.

"I've already said I want to choose the music for the ceremony and first dance. I will also organise the honeymoon, I want the day to be about you, so you know how special you are to me."

"Okay, I would prefer to plan it with Mandy rather than a wedding planner."

He gets up and gives me a kiss. "Over to you then, my Chuddly, I can't wait for the day. I best do some work now though, let's go out for some lunch later."

"Okay, I will clear the table." Standing, I give him a kiss.

Bradley heads out of the kitchen and I load the plates into the dishwasher. Grabbing a pad and pen, I settle on the sofa, turn on some eighties music, and start writing ideas for the wedding. After a few hours, there is a knock at the front door of the house. I get off the sofa and open the door. A guy in his late teens is standing there staring at me. He looks kind of familiar but I'm not sure where I've seen him before.

"Can I help you?" I ask.

His cheeks flush, his stance hunched and awkward. "I'm looking for Bradley Franklin."

"Hold on, I will get him." I turn back into the house and shout out to Bradley to come downstairs, then turn back to face the guy.

"What is it?" Bradley asks as he walks down the stairs.

"This young guy wants to speak to you. Sorry, I didn't get your name."

"Danny," he mumbles and looks sheepishly at

Bradley, "Danny Brooks." The colour drains from Bradley's face and he grabs hold of my arm to steady himself as the words leave his mouth. Seeing them face to face I realise why he looks familiar.

"I'm your son."

28

*B*radley grips my arm tight as I stand and frantically stare between the two of them, the silence adding to the tension. I'm frozen with shock as my skin chills to the bone, I'm unsure how to react. I cannot tell if it is my body trembling or Bradley's, as he is standing so close. Danny is staring directly into Bradley's eyes, the tears welling in his own. The intense emotions of the moment are overwhelming us all. It's like watching a family reunion on TV, only this is real and it's happening right in front of me with the man I love.

After what feels like an eternity Bradley speaks. "Come in." His voice is shaky and broken as he tries to gather himself.

Danny steps into the house, his head held low as Bradley leads him into the lounge. Closing the front door, I lean back against it, my heart beating erratically, tears welling as my own emotions break. I take deep breaths, trying to stay in control for Bradley. My legs are trembling as I walk towards the lounge. Standing by the door, I'm unsure if I should stay or leave them to talk as they stare at each other from opposite sofas.

"I'm sorry, I did not know, your mother never mentioned—" Bradley rambles, his words stuttering from his mouth.

"It's okay, I know she never told you," Danny interrupts, his voice the most confident of us all. "She only told me the truth about you and what happened when I turned eighteen. All the time I was growing up she had told me you left her when I was young. After six months of deliberating, I tried to find you."

I watch Bradley, the mix of emotions showing in his eyes. "I don't know what to say. If I had known about you, I would have been there for you," Bradley says, his voice still quivering with the shock.

Danny stands up. "I should go. I'm sorry, I know it is a shock," he blurts out. Tears flood down his cheeks.

Bradley stands and grabs his arm as he walks towards the door, pulling him into his arms, he hugs him tight as both their tears flow. I wipe my own eyes with the back of my hand, the release of tension hitting me as I watch them reunite.

"Do you want me to leave you alone for a while?" I hesitantly ask not wanting to interrupt them.

Bradley looks at me over Danny's shoulder. "If you're sure you don't mind."

"No, I think you two need time to talk," I say, catching my breath and trying to look confident and in control, although I'm falling apart inside.

"Okay, thanks," Bradley says, still hugging Danny as he sobs into his shoulder.

I get my phone and keys, put on my trainers, and leave the house without saying goodbye. It's a grey overcast day and the damp air hits my face as I close the door. I walk along the street; the cold intensifies on my face, wet from my tears as my mind runs into overdrive. How will this affect our relationship, what about the wedding plans? I take my phone out of my pocket and scroll through the names, pressing on Mandy's.

"Hello, honey, how're things going? Don't tell me you've had another big idea for the wedding." Her voice is chirpy.

"Mandy, Bradley's son just turned up at the house." My voice breaks as my eyes well up again the phone shaking in my hand.

"What! Oh my God, I didn't know he had a son," she says, the tone in her voice rapidly changing.

"No. neither did he, I left them at the house to talk."

"David, I don't know what to say."

"I'm totally gobsmacked, I don't know what to do. I dealt with the shock about his wedding to a woman, but this, what will this do to our relationship?" I ramble down the phone without taking a breath.

"Oh, come on, you, don't go jumping to conclusions. Yes, it's a shock, but I'm sure it won't change your plans. You need to concentrate on Bradley, he'll need your support, I can't even imagine how he's feeling just finding out he has a son. To have missed all the years with him. He must be in turmoil."

"You're right, he will need my support," I reply, her words making me stop and think.

"Yes, stop worrying about you and him, I'm sure your relationship will be fine. Focus on helping him through this shock."

"You're always right, Mandy. What would I do without you?"

"Always getting in a muddle, that's what you would do. Now have a walk get yourself together, then go home and take care of Bradley. He will need you more now than ever."

"I will."

"Okay, message me later and let me know how things are."

"Will do, thanks."

I hang up the phone and continue walking down to the river. Standing at the edge I watch the river boats chug along, people laughing and enjoying themselves as I turn my thoughts to Bradley. What must he be feeling? My eyes well up again as I think about all the things he would have missed. Danny's first words, seeing him walk, his first day at school, the list is endless. How could his ex-wife do that to him?

My head is all over the place, poor Danny thinking Bradley had deserted him for years only to find out he knew nothing about him. What a mess. I hope they can recuperate something from it all. I'm wishing I had put a jacket on the wind along the river has a chill to it as it hits my skin. Mandy is right; this is the time to stop thinking about myself and be there for Bradley.

My phone rings, pulling it out my pocket I see Bradley's smiling face on the screen.

"Hello," I say in a shallow voice, unsure what he will say.

"Hi, Danny has gone. Can you come back home?"

"Yes, I'm on my way."

He says nothing else before hanging up the phone.

I rush back to the house as quick as I can, desperate to give Bradley a hug.

As I close the door, Bradley walks out of the lounge, his eyes raw from crying. Reaching out, he touches the side of my face, his eyes full of sorrow as they connect with mine. I try to hold back my tears; I want to be strong for him. He pulls me tight into his arms, his face snuggles against my neck. The wetness of his skin is cool against mine; I have never seen him so torn and vulnerable. I wrap my arms around him and crush him tighter. Neither of us speak; the closeness and warmth of our embrace says everything. The clock ticking on the wall is the only thing to break the silence.

"Are you okay?" I ask, my voice shaking.

"I think so, I wasn't expecting that." His voice sounds as broken as he looks.

"I know, neither of us were," I say, my hand stroking down his back. "Did you have a good talk?"

"Yes, we agreed to meet up in a few days. Thank you for giving us time to talk."

"Don't be silly, you needed the space."

"Thank you," he says. His lips touch mine, placing the softest, sweetest kiss on them. "Let's have a drink, I need one and I will tell you what he said."

"Are you sure you want to talk about it?"

"David, you're my world now, I want to talk to you." There's a hint of anger to his voice.

His words make my body tingle, he gives me another quick kiss and heads to the kitchen. I follow him and watch as he pours vodka into a glass and drinks it in one swallow before refilling two glasses and adding lemonade this time. He hands me a glass.

"I can't believe she kept him a secret from me for all these years." I stare at him in silence and sip my drink, unsure what to say, giving him the chance to speak.

"Fucking bitch!" he shouts and throws his glass into the sink, it shatters against the basin. As he turns and grips the counter, his back towards me, he cries. His body shakes with anger. I put my glass on the table and run over to him, hugging him from behind, not speaking but letting him know I'm there for him.

"I'm sorry," he says between his tears. I turn him to face me.

"You need not be sorry, you have every reason to be angry," I say as tears run down my cheeks.

We hug each other tight as he sobs into my shoulder, his breathing finally calming as his body slowly relaxes. This is the first time I have seen him so upset. The ordinarily confident man shattered by this morning's events.

"I've missed so much of his life," he whispers.

"But now you have him in your life, you can show him what a wonderful dad you would have been and will be from now on."

"Thank you," he says, kissing me. "I know this must be hard for you."

"Don't worry about me. I want you to be happy, because when you're happy, I'm happy," I say.

He kisses me softly. "This won't change our plans, I hope you know that," he says.

"Yeah, I know." I hug him tight, snuggling my head into his neck, relieved and reassured by his words and the warmth of his body.

"Let me get you another drink. Sit on the sofa, we can chat there," I say.

He gives me another kiss and walks out of the kitchen. I quickly clear away the broken glass and pour two more drinks.

Bradley is sitting on the sofa, still looking very vulnerable and upset. I hand him a glass and sit beside him.

"So how was Danny?"

"It relieved him that I was glad to see him. He has been worrying for days about what my reaction would be, apart from the initial shock of finding out I have a son."

"Good. He seems like a nice lad."

"His mother kept the truth about me a secret for many years until he was sixteen. When she was hospitalised after a car accident, she finally admitted the truth to him because she feared the worst for herself and did not want him to be left on his own."

"So, he has known for a few years then."

"Yeah, but once she got out of hospital, he didn't want to upset her with questions about me, so he kept quiet about it. Until he turned eighteen, then he asked her to tell him the whole truth. She admitted finding out she was pregnant shortly after we had split and decided not to tell me. Because she was bitter and angry with me about what happened between us."

I place my hand on his leg and smile at him. "Well the past is the past as you say. Now you can make a future with him."

"How do you feel about me having a son?"

"Bradley, I would love you if you had ten kids, nothing will change how I feel about you. We're getting married and I'm happy Danny will be part of our lives."

"Thank you." He leans over and kisses me. "I love you, David."

"I love you too."

We spent two hours talking about Danny and the wedding. Bradley seems to have calmed down, reiterating he would meet up with Danny in a few days to have a good chat.

"You know what I could do with now?" he says, the look in his eyes saying more than the words.

"Downstairs?" I ask.

"Yes, come with me." He stands up and pulls me up from the sofa, hugging me tight to him, giving me a kiss. I feel his cock pressing hard into my leg, so I grind myself against him. Taking my hand, he leads me to the door of the basement.

Opening the door, I follow him down the stairs, the anticipation already building inside me. The chill in the air makes my skin tingle and makes goosebumps rise on my arms. I want to please him to help relieve his tension and this is the place, this is where he is the master.

He leads me over towards the bed. I stand facing

him, a few feet from the bed, as he sits down on the edge of the mattress.

"Strip naked." His voice is loud and commanding as he watches me.

I pull my T-shirt off over my head and my nipples stiffen from the chill. My chest and belly are hairless and my skin is smooth, just how Bradley likes. His eyes flicker up and down my body as he watches me. I slide my joggers and boxers to the floor, bending over to remove them from my feet.

Standing naked, my cock stiffens as I look at him, waiting for his next command.

"Come here." The low growl in his voice turns me on even more as I walk and stand directly in front of him. My cock is inches from his face hard, throbbing pre-cum leaking from the head.

He grabs my arse cheeks and pulls me forward making my cock head touch his lips. His tongue licks the pre-cum leaking from the head. I stifle my moans of pleasure, knowing in this room I can only make a noise when he gives me permission.

His mouth opens as he pulls me closer, the warmth of his wet mouth and tongue feel good as it closes around my cock, sliding down my shaft. I stare down at him, my hands clasped behind my back as he licks and sucks my cock, his hands gripping my arse so I cannot move. I want to push my cock deeper into his throat, but I know he is in control. He releases my cock from his mouth, throbbing and wet, and the cool air tingles against my skin.

"Lay across my lap," he orders.

Edging back on the bed so I can lie across his legs. My hard cock presses tight against his leg as he moves me into the best position. My arms stretch onto the bed, my cock throbbing and leaking onto his leg as I anticipate what he will do.

The sound of the first hard slap echoes around the room as his hand hits my backside. The burning on my skin quickly cools from the air in the room. I bury my face into the bed to smother my moans of pain and pleasure, while my cock stiffens more. I wince in pain as his hand hits me again and again. My skin burns hotter with each slap. My cock throbs with excitement and leaks as it rubs against his leg. He smacks me harder and faster, releasing his tension; his breathing becoming erratic as he loses control. I've wanted him to spank me for so long and this is how I dreamed it would feel. My arse cheeks burn fiercely; the cool air of the room no longer eases the pain.

One more loud smack and I can't hold back anymore. My cock explodes, shooting cum against his leg as I roar into the bed, still trying to stifle the sound.

He pushes me off his legs and stands up. "Lay face down on the bed," he shouts.

I clamber to the centre of the bed lying face down I know my arse must glow as my skin is burning like hell. Looking back towards him, he strips off his clothes. His cock is hard as he removes his underwear then climbs back on the bed, straddling my arse. I hear him spit into his hand; the wet fingers feel great as they glide over my hole a single finger pushing into me. Then I feel his cock press against me. My arse relaxes, allowing him to slide deep inside. I hear him growl as I feel his pubic hair brush against my burning cheeks. His cock throbs deep inside me as he lowers himself onto my back. His hairy chest presses me to the bed as he grinds his cock into me. He bites the side of my neck as his thrusts get faster, pounding his cock deep into my arse.

I continue to stifle my moans of pleasure as he fucks me harder, his breathing heavy and deep in my ears, I can tell he is nearing the edge. Pushing my arse up from the bed as he pushes down into me, I try to get his cock as deep in me as I can. Then he growls loudly in my ear as his body convulses against mine, his cock throbbing inside me as his warm cum fills my hole.

He collapses on my back, panting for breath, his body sweating against mine as he relaxes.

I smile to myself, feeling satisfied that I have helped relieve his tension of the day. After a while, he rolls off my back and lies next to me.

"I needed that," he says, still breathing heavy.

"So, did I," I reply, giving him a kiss before I snuggle into him and lay my head on his hairy chest.

He wraps his arms around me and pulls me tight to his chest. As we both drift off to sleep.

29

Four days later

*M*andy and I head to the pub after work for a drink and catch up; it's difficult talking in work there're always too many ears about.

"Grab a seat, I'll get a bottle to share," I say, pointing to a table opposite the door.

"Okay," she replies, taking her jacket off.

The barman smiles at me as he takes my order. "Take a seat, I'll bring it over, we're not busy tonight," he says.

"Thanks, babe."

I take my jacket off and sit at the table.

"So, how's Bradley coping?" she asks.

"Okay, I think. He was really angry initially, but seems a lot calmer now. He's meeting up with Danny this evening."

"Oh, good, the wedding plans still on track?"

"Yeah, we found a lovely Manor house that holds

ceremonies and they will host the reception afterwards. Can you come with us on Sunday and have a look at the place?"

"Yeah, definitely, once the venue is sorted, we can look into all the trimmings," she says.

The barman puts the bottle of wine and glasses on the table, giving me a wink as he walks away.

"Yep, I still can't believe I'm getting married in November."

"It's so exciting," she says, smiling as she pours the wine.

"I really want it to be a special day for both of us; I think Bradley needs it after recent events."

"He does indeed. Has he told you anything about the honeymoon yet?"

"No, he's keeping that very close to his chest. Whenever I ask, he says it's the beginning of our new life together."

"I wonder what he has planned," she says, the excitement ringing out in her voice.

We chat away for an hour; a few more people have come into the pub but it is still relatively empty. I take a sip of my wine as my body freezes and a mixture of fear, anticipation flows through me. My ex, Craig, walks into the pub with another guy.

Mandy must have seen my expression change. "What's wrong," she says turning to look towards the door. "Oh, what is he doing here?" Her detest of Craig is clear in the tone of her voice.

Craig sees me and walks over the other guy following. "Hey, stranger, a long time since I've seen you," he says as though we are best friends.

"Hi, yeah, it has been." My voice is shallow, my demeanour changing in his presence.

"This is Michael," he says, introducing the chubby guy next to him, he looks like a slightly older version of me, only balding.

"Hey," I say with a little smile. He smiles back but doesn't speak. I recognise the look on his face, the same fear I had around Craig, never sure whether to speak to people so I didn't upset him.

"What have you been up to?" Craig asks.

"He's getting married," Mandy cuts in the conversation.

"Oh, really," he replies.

"Yes, in November to my partner Bradley," I mumble and look down at the table, still affected by his presence.

"Wow, that's a surprise," Craig says.

"Yes, and we're just discussing the plans, so if you don't mind," Mandy says turning her back to him.

"Okay, maybe will catch up later," Craig says, giving me a wink as he walks to the other side of the bar, Michael following him.

"Why does he still get to you?" She asks.

"It's hard to explain," I reply. "The energy just drained from my body the moment I saw him."

"He can't hurt you anymore."

"I know, but the damage is already done," I say, my eyes welling up.

"Come on, let's get back to the wedding, ignore that low life."

"Okay, what do you think of white horses and a pink carriage?" I say, trying to lighten my mood and take my thoughts away from Craig.

"I think Bradley would have something to say about that," she says with an exaggerated laugh, obviously for Craig's benefit.

We continue chatting and discussing the wedding, I can't resist looking over at Craig and Michael now and then. They are all over each other in the corner. Craig catches me looking at him and gives me a smile. I turn away, drinking my wine as quickly as I can. Once we finish the bottle, we head home. I give Mandy a kiss and hug outside the pub and take a slow walk back home. My thoughts turning to how Bradley would have got on with Danny today. I'm really hoping they can make things work after all these missed years.

I get home before Bradley. Making myself a coffee, I sit on the sofa, waiting for him to get home. My thoughts turn back to Craig and how it made me feel seeing him. Now that I'm with Bradley I realise how controlling he was, how he fucked with my head, twisting everything I said, making me feel bad if I ever questioned anything he did. He was handsome and charming, but he had a nasty side nobody ever saw, except me, behind closed doors. I could tell from Michael's reaction that he's now living the life I led for so many years.

It's true what they say about relationships, unless you're in it, you never know what's going on between people. As I ponder my past, I hear the front door opening.

"Hey, I'm in here," I call out.

Bradley appears at the doorway to the lounge. "Why are you sitting in the dark?" he asks.

"Just thinking about things."

He switches on the light. "Did you have a good evening with Mandy?"

"Yeah, it was nice. We discussed ideas for the wedding and I invited her along to look at the venue on Sunday."

"Good, I'm sure she'll love it."

"How did things go with Danny?"

"Very well, thanks. He told me about some things he has done whilst growing up. He even brought along some photos of him over the years for me to keep."

"That's lovely," I reply, my hands locked around the coffee mug. "Would you like a coffee?"

"It's okay, I'll grab one. Stay there, I will be back in a minute."

He disappears from view, whistling happily as he walks to the kitchen. I'm so pleased things seem to be working out between him and Danny. Within a view minutes he returns with his coffee and slumps on the sofa next to me.

"What's wrong?" he asks.

"Nothing, I was just thinking that's all."

"You're not still worrying about Danny and our future."

"No not at all," I reply, trying to sound a little upbeat.

"What is it then? I know something is wrong."

"Okay, Craig turned up at the pub this evening."

"Oh, did he say anything to you?"

"He came over and said hello, but Mandy soon brushed him away."

"Good for her, so why are you so glum?"

"I don't know, just being around him really affects my mood."

He reaches out and touches the side of my face. "He is your past now, we have each other and nothing will come between us. Try to forget him, focus on our future, he is just a bad memory."

"Yeah, you're right." I lean over and kiss him. "Thanks."

"So, tell me about the wedding plans."

We chat for a while, I tell him about the plans and he seems happy with them. Talking about the wedding also lifts my spirits again. He tells me more about his evening with Danny, the smile on his face as he speaks about his son is lovely to see and chokes me up a little.

"It's late, we best head to bed," he says.

"Yeah, leave the mugs, I will wash them up in the morning."

He stands up and takes my hand. Pulling me up from the sofa, he embraces me, kissing me passionately.

"I love you, mister, and I can't wait to marry you," he says with a smile.

"I love you too," I reply as we stare deep into each other's eyes. I feel his cock stiffen against my leg.

"Good, let's hit the sack."

30

Sunday

*T*he doorbell rings, I open the door and Mandy is standing on the step.

"All ready for the day," she says a huge smile on her face.

"Yes, I'm so excited! Come in."

Bradley has come to the hallway as Mandy walks in, he gives her a kiss, as I close the door.

"I don't know what I will be like on the day of the wedding; I'm so excited about visiting the venue," she says.

"So is he; it's all he's spoken about since he got up this morning," Bradley says.

"Don't act so cool, you are as well," I say, playfully smacking his arm.

"Yes, of course I am," he replies, giving me a cheeky smile. "Well, get your shoes on, the car is outside."

"Car," Mandy says.

"We have a chauffeur to take us there; you should know what he's like by now," I say.

"Nothing wrong with a little luxury now and then," he says, his irresistible smile gleaming across his face.

We leave the house and Bradley opens the door for Mandy and I to get in the executive car.

"This is posh," Mandy says as she gets comfortable.

"Yes, it is nice, but we could have driven in your car," I reply.

"Stop grumbling, I know you enjoy it really," Bradley says as he gets into the car.

I laugh and smile at him, he knows me too well. The drive to the venue in Buckinghamshire takes a while because of traffic but we make the most of the time chatting and drinking Champagne in the car.

We arrive at the entrance gates to the Manor House. As the car drives along the sweeping driveway towards the house, my heart skips a beat with excitement. It is as lovely as it looked in the photos on the website.

"Oh, it looks stunning," Mandy says and we smile at each other.

The brickwork of the building is grey and aged. Two stone pillars hold the canopy over the entrance. Heavy wooden painted black doors with large brass door-knockers are framed by white stone. Wisteria climbing plants carefully cut around the lower bay windows on either side of the entrance. The car stops outside the entrance and we all get out, stepping onto the grey gravel drive.

"What do you think?" Bradley asks.

"I love it," I say, the excitement clear in my voice.

"Yes, it's wonderful," Mandy says.

The smell of the rhododendrons is lingering sweetly in the air as we all look up at the towering house before us. A large pot on either side of the steps bursts with colour. The house has three floors, open balconies sit above the bay windows.

"Shall we have a look around?" Bradley asks.

"Yep, definitely," I reply entwining my fingers between his, we hold hands as we follow Mandy up the seven stone steps to the door.

As we reach the top of the stairs, the doors swing open, two young men in black uniforms hold them open and gesture us inside. An older lady in an elegant purple dress greets us as we walk into the house.

"Welcome to Heston House," she says, smiling and pushing her silver-rimmed glasses back onto her nose. "I'm Penelope."

"I'm Bradley, this is David and Mandy."

"Pleased to meet you," she says interlocking her hands across the front of her body as she nods politely at us.

"Thank you," Bradley replies a formal tone to his voice. Both Mandy and I just smile politely.

"I will give you a tour of the building. Please ask questions as we walk around, then you can have a look around the grounds at your leisure and discuss your plans."

"That sounds perfect," Bradley says.

"Good, follow me, we can start in the ceremony room."

I grip Bradley's hand tighter, trying to contain my

excitement as we follow her down a corridor. Opening a large black door to her right, she leads us into the ceremony room.

"Wow," Mandy says as she steps inside.

I catch my breath at how beautiful the room is, with its ornate white plastered walls. Four grey stone pillars support the ceiling and rows of silver chairs face towards a large archway at the front of the room.

"The arch is where the ceremony takes place, you can have the room decorated with flowers or material dressings, however you choose. We have two companies I can recommend, but you are free to use anyone. We can set the seating for up to two-hundred and fifty guests," she says.

My heart is pounding with excitement as the reality of our wedding taking place here hits me. Bradley squeezes my hand, sending shivers down my spine. I want to get married right here and now.

"We have two dining rooms that can be used for either a sit-down meal or buffet," she says and gestures us back out of the room. Walking further along the corridor she opens a door to her left this time. "Do you know if you will have a sit-down meal?"

Bradley looks at me and raises his eyebrows, prompting me to answer.

"Yes, it will be a sit-down meal," I reply, my cheeks burn a little as she smiles at me.

Inside, the room is set with several round tables and a large long oblong table at one end. Large, open gold curtains hang heavy against the arched windows, allowing light to flood into the room. Wooden panelling clads the other walls. The tables are covered in white cloth with silver chairs placed around them.

"As with the ceremony room, you can have this room decorated to your own choice of colours," she says.

"How many people can be seated in here?" Bradley asks. Both Mandy and I are too awestruck by the beauty of the place to speak.

"This is the larger dining room and can hold one hundred and fifty guests. The smaller room holds one hundred and twenty. If you wish to seat up to two hundred and fifty, we have marquees available."

"Okay, thank you."

She gives Bradley a quirky smile and gestures us back out of the room. We follow her to the end of the corridor and she opens another door on the left, leading us outside two large marquees have been erected on the grass.

"The marquees can be used for both dining and evening entertainment," she says as we follow her into the closest one.

People were inside, busy decorating the walls with white and pink flowers. We had a quick look, then followed her back into the house along another corridor, out the back of the house, and onto a large patio area that overlooks the grounds. The gardens look immaculate perfect for the wedding photos.

"I will leave you to have a look around the grounds. If you choose the venue you would have exclusive access to everything including the guest rooms for twenty-four hours. I will be in the reception area if you have any further questions or wish to discuss a booking," she says, smiling she gives us a little nod.

"Thank you," Bradley says as she walks away.

"Well, what do you think?" he asks.

"I love it, I want to get married today."

Bradley laughs, "Mandy?"

"It's beautiful; the rooms and the grounds are all stunning."

"So, are we all agreed? This is the place?"

"Yes," both Mandy and I reply at the same time.

"Okay, wait here, and I will check if it's available for our date."

Bradley gives me a kiss and walks away.

"Mandy, I can't believe I will get married here."

"You deserve it," she says giving me a hug.

Bradley returns after a while, his face looking solemn as he walks towards us. My heart is thudding in my chest preparing myself for a disappointment.

"It's all ours," he says pulling me into his arms and kissing me, "the date is set for Saturday 24th of November."

I look at Mandy and she is welling up. "Don't; you will make me cry," I say.

"I'm sorry, I'm just so pleased for you both, come here."

She opens her arms and we join in a group hug.

"Oh my God, we're getting married," I shout.

"We are, and they set the date."

I can't even explain the excitement I'm feeling now. The buzz of excitement staying with me for the rest of the day.

One month later

"*I* will think about you at work today," I say and give Bradley a kiss.

"I know you will, but don't worry, I'm sure the day will go okay."

"Well, if it seems right, give Danny my love."

"I will, now you better scoot or you will be late for work," he says and gives my backside a slap.

"I hope there's more of that to come later."

"If you're a good boy, now get to work."

I give him a long, lingering kiss. "Have a good day," I say as I pick up my rucksack for work.

"You too," he says, opening the door so I can leave.

I give him a smile as he closes the door behind me. He always seems nervous about meeting with Danny, which I can understand, they have a lot of time to catch up on.

It's a sunny day and I hum to myself as I walk to

work. I'm eager for the day to be over so I can find out about Bradley's day.

The working day seems to drag and my patience has been short on the phones today. Harry, my manager, pulled me up twice about my attitude on calls. My thoughts are elsewhere today and the job is getting on my nerves a little, listening to people constantly moaning or demanding what they want. I was glad when the clock reached five. Grabbing my rucksack, I rushed home as quick as I could.

Bradley is not back yet, so I prepare him a pasta bake, I can put in the oven when he gets home. I'm sure he will be exhausted when he gets back. My thoughts focus on him and Danny again and I get anxious about how they will have gotten along.

I'm cleaning the mess I've made in the kitchen when I hear the front door open.

"Hi, honey, I'm home," Bradley calls out in a chirpy voice.

"I'm in the kitchen, sweetheart," I reply, relieved to hear his happy voice.

Bradley has a huge smile on his face as he walks into the kitchen, a little unsteady on his feet.

"Have we had a drink?" I ask as he gets closer.

"Just a few, my gorgeous man," he replies and pulls me into him. Wrapping his arms around me, he places a soft kiss on my lips, the smell of alcohol is overpowering.

"Well, I'm sure you deserved it. How did the day go with Danny?"

"I will tell you everything in a bit, but I need a piss now," he says and rushes upstairs.

"Charming, I'm cooking a pasta bake," I call after him.

By the time he comes back to the kitchen I have poured us both a glass of wine. I hand him his glass, "So, tell me about your day."

"Firstly, I must give you some news," he says, the slight slur to his voice turns me on and my cock twitches.

"What's that?"

"I have my best man."

"Oh, who have you decided on?"

"Danny; he wants to be at the wedding."

"Oh, Bradley, that's fantastic news." I can feel myself choking up with emotion. "I'm so pleased."

"I'm chuffed," he says, the tears building in his eyes.

Leaning forward, I give him a kiss. "It will be a brilliant day."

"Yes, it couldn't be any more perfect."

"Take a seat, I will get dinner out of the oven."

We eat dinner and Bradley tells me more about his day with Danny. It is wonderful to hear they are getting along so well. After dinner we sit on the sofa in the lounge chatting more, Bradley's voice slurring the more he drinks the wine.

"I think we should head up to bed, before you fall asleep down here," I say.

"You're probably right," he says. Trying to stand up, he sways and stumbles; I stand up and hold him steady.

"I love you, David," he says and kisses me.

"I love you too, now let's get upstairs."

Helping him up to the bedroom, he sits on the edge

of the bed laughing to himself as he tries to lift his feet to take his socks off.

I watch him for a while, laughing along with him and admiring my handsome man. After a short while, I help him get undressed and into bed. As soon as his head hits the pillow, he is in a deep sleep. I undress and climb into bed, snuggling in behind him. I run my fingers through his chest hair and rest my head against the nape of his neck before falling off to sleep.

I wake up before Bradley; we have kicked the quilt off the bed during the night. He is lying on his back, his cock hard and pointing towards the ceiling. I shuffle on the bed, edging my face close to his cock, my own is hard and leaking as I grip his shaft gently, lowering my mouth over the head. I hear him moan as my tongue circles the head, slowly pushing his foreskin back. His cock slides deeper into my mouth as he shifts on the bed.

I feel his mouth warm and wet as it closes over the head of my cock and I let out a loud moan of pleasure. Shifting on top of him my thighs grip his head as his mouth licks and sucks my cock.

Sliding my mouth down the length of his shaft I hear his muffled moans as I take him deep in my throat. Gently squeezing his balls as I suck him. His balls tighten against his body as my tongue circles the head of his cock.

Knowing he is about to shoot into my mouth sends me over the edge. I buck against his face, trying to push my cock as deep in his mouth as I can, releasing my load.

He responds pushing up from the bed, his cock

exploding in my mouth. I suck and lick him clean before rolling off and shifting back up the bed to face him.

"Morning, gorgeous," I say.

"Morning, Chuddly," he replies pulling me into his chest.

We lie cuddling together a little, breathless from the morning wake up action.

"It's great news about Danny being at the wedding."

"Yes, I'm so pleased he will be there; it will make the day extra special."

"It will indeed," I reply. He kisses me softy on the top of my head, making me cuddle in tighter into his chest. "I still can't believe we're getting married, when I think back to where I was in life last year before we met."

"You need to move on from the past. Think about us and our future." He strokes his fingers through my hair.

"I know, but it's difficult forgetting when I was in such a bad place. Being with you has made me realise how bad it really was."

"I will make sure you have so many nice memories of things we do together. You won't have room in your head for any negative thoughts about your past."

Laughing at his comment, I say, "You're so lovely."

"When you're my husband, we will travel the world together. I'm never going to let you go, my Chuddly."

Shifting on the bed, I straddle him and look down into his eyes. "I never want to be without you."

"You won't be," he replies before pulling me down to kiss me.

"We better get up, there's still lots to sort out before the wedding."

"Five minutes more," he says. His adorable smile wins me over easily.

"Okay."

I lay down onto him and he hugs me tight.

32

Three weeks later

The alarm sounds. I roll over and snuggle into Bradley as he reaches to switch it off.

"What time is it?" my voice croaky from the sleep.

"Four-thirty. I've got to get to the airport, the flight to Valencia is at eight."

"Oh yeah, I wish I was coming with you," I say, kissing the side of his neck as I slide my leg between his.

"Why don't you come along?" he asks.

"I've got work today."

"Phone and say you're not well, come with me to Valencia," he says, the tone in his voice very serious. He turns and kisses me.

"I wouldn't be able to get a flight now, and even if I could, imagine how much they would charge."

He reaches over and picks up his phone, quickly searching on the flight checker app. "There are seats available, you have a passport, come with me."

"You're being serious," I say, suddenly alert at his suggestion.

"Totally, I don't like being away from you, come to Valencia with me, once my meetings are over, we will have all evening together to enjoy the city."

"Really, how much is the flight?"

"It is a special fiancé rate," he replies with a smile. "Come on pack a bag." He kicks the quilt off us and smacks my arse before standing up. "Get a move on the car will be here soon, we're going to Valencia."

I roll onto my back and stare at him. "Are you being serious?"

"Yes, get moving. We don't want to miss the flight."

Clambering off the bed, we shower together and get dressed. Whilst I throw a few things into a rucksack, as it will be an overnight stay, Bradley books my flight, ensuring we have seats together on the plane. Within thirty minutes, we are both ready at the front door.

"I can't believe I'm going with you," I say.

"Get used to it, sweetheart, this is what you're signing up for."

He pulls me hard against him, pressing his warm lips to mine, his tongue pushing into my mouth. His kiss is deep and passionate as he hugs me tight.

"I would spend all my time with you if I could," I say.

"Good, that's what I want to hear."

A knock at the door startles me.

"Come on then," he says as he opens the door. The familiar driver and black executive car are outside.

"Morning, Sir," the driver says.

"Morning," we reply, Bradley locks the front door of the house as I get into the car.

"I will have to phone work from Valencia," I say as the car pulls away from the house.

"I'm sure you will be able to make an excuse to have the day off," he says followed by a cheeky laugh.

Smiling at him I lean over and give him a quick kiss.

It doesn't take long to get to the airport; there's not much traffic this early in the morning. We go to the business check-in desk and the assistant hands us our boarding cards. Then I follow Bradley to the first-class lounge where we have breakfast and wait for the flight.

The flight was great, with a nice meal and several glasses of Champagne. I arrive in Valencia a little light headed. We get a taxi to the hotel. During the ride, I make a quick call to work, telling my manager, Harry, I have an upset stomach and not to expect me in for two days. Once we are checked in at reception, we head up to the room. Bradley gives me a kiss and leaves me in the hotel suite to have a sleep whilst he goes to his meetings.

The door to the suite opening disturbs me.

"Afternoon, sleepy head," Bradley says as he walks into the bedroom.

"What's the time? I must have dropped off."

"It's one o'clock, did you have a good sleep?" he asks. Sitting on the bed next to me, he slides his hand over my chest and smiles down at me.

"I must have been comfortable, how were the meetings?"

"All good, we will exceed our targets in the Spanish sector this year."

"Good." I lay staring up at him. Moving my hand, I grab his hand and lift it to my lips, placing a gentle kiss on the back of his hand.

"As much as I would love to strip off and climb in bed with you, we only have this afternoon and evening to see some city highlights. We fly back at eight in the morning."

"This is a very quick trip."

"I've cut all my trips as short as I can so I can spend more time at home with you," he says before leaning down and kissing me.

"That's lovely."

"Now get up and get dressed so I can show around the city."

I clamber off the bed and get dressed whilst Bradley changes into casual clothes. We have one last hug and kiss before leaving the hotel.

I'm surprised how warm it is outside considering how cold it was when we left London. Our hotel is situated next to a park.

"This park used to be the Turia river that ran though the city. In 1957 there were heavy rains which caused the river to overflow, flooding into the city. Following that disaster, they rerouted the river outside of the city and the whole Turia riverbed was changed into one long park," Bradley says as we walk through the park.

"It is a beautiful park."

"Next time we come here, we will stay longer and you can see the whole park and the various sections that change along its length."

"I would love that."

We spend a few hours walking around the city and Bradley tells me the history of various buildings. He makes me smile, giving me all the detail like he is a local tour guide. Ending up in the Carmen district of the city, I follow him along the back streets to a small restaurant tucked away down the end of a side street.

The restaurant is small inside with large heavy wooden tables set against the black painted walls. A short plump lady dressed in black approaches us as we walk through the door.

"Buenas tardes, senor Franklin, es maravilloso verte de nuevo," she says with a smile.

Bradley kisses her once on each cheek. "Buenas tardes, Maria. Podemos tener una mesa para dos por favor," Bradley replies, his Spanish rolling fluently.

"Si, por supuesto." She directs us to a table and we sit down.

"I never knew you could speak Spanish," I say.

"Knowing the basics of a few languages helps with the business. I love this restaurant, I come here whenever I am in Valencia. Maria doesn't speak English, this is a real Spanish place, and the food is wonderful."

Maria returns with the menus which are also all written in Spanish with no English translations. So, I have to rely on Bradley to tell me what is on the menu. I choose my food as Maria places an ice bucket with a bottle of pink Prosecco in it on the table. She takes the food orders from Bradley in Spanish and smiles politely before walking away.

"This is a lovely choice of restaurant; it has a warm, homey feel to the place."

"I always look forward to coming here. My first visit was many years ago, and I struggled to order my food. Leaving both me and Maria laughing as we tried to understand each other through stuttered words and hand signals. Ever since then, this has been my favourite restaurant," he says as he pours our drinks.

"Cheers," we both say at the same time.

Whilst we chat away about the wedding plans. Maria brings over the first course of food, which looks amazing and tastes just as wonderful.

"Are you glad you came along?"

"Yes, I still feel bad letting my friends at work down, though, as they will have a lot more calls to answer without me."

"Why don't you give it up? You really need not work or worry about money now. Let's be honest, you don't really like the job."

"I know, but it wouldn't feel right to have you working and me doing nothing."

"Well, do some work for me, just something part time to get you out of the house. At least then you can come away with me anytime."

"That's tempting, but let's see how things go."

"You still have that underlying insecurity. I wish I could convince you otherwise."

"I'm sorry, I don't want you to think I don't trust you."

Bradley smiles. "I know it's not that, Craig has a lot to answer for, my little Chuddly."

His words bring a smile back to my face as we enjoy the rest of the dinner. We are both feeling tired and a little light-headed by the time we leave the restaurant. With an early flight in the morning, we decide it's best to head back to the hotel to sleep.

33

Three days before the wedding

"I hope you will be a good boy at your stag party tonight," Bradley says.

"Well, I might have to make the most of my last few nights of freedom. There might be some handsome hunk at the bar," I reply with a giggle.

Bradley pulls me into his arms. "Not long now and I will be able to call you husband," he says, his eyes fixed on mine. "You will be good."

I kiss him softly. "No one could take your place."

"Good, now hurry, you don't want to be late for your own party."

"I wish you were coming along," I say, heading to the door.

"That's not tradition, besides I have already had mine. This is your celebration with your friends."

"Very true. I will miss you though."

"I will miss you too," he says before giving me

another quick kiss and smacking my arse. "Now, go, enjoy yourself." He holds the door open as I walk down the steps.

Mandy said to arrive at the bar for seven o'clock. Strangely, nobody is standing outside as they usually do. I walk to the door and pull it open. The song *Congratulations* burst out of the sound system as I step into the bar. They have decorated the place in pink and white balloons. All the regulars are in the bar; Mandy, Brian and Tony rush over. They throw a pink sash over my head and as it drops across my chest, I can see the words *Soon to be Married Shag Me Now* written on it. Mandy places a *Kiss Me Quick* hat on my head and hands me a glass of Prosecco, before kissing me on each cheek.

"Congratulations, David, I don't know who is more excited, me or you?"

"Definitely me, babes, I can't believe I'm get married in three days. I'm so excited!"

"I know," Mandy says, clapping her hands with excitement.

"It should have been me that night, sweetie, remember I saw him first," Brian says with a smile.

"Yeah, but he likes his men chunky, babes." I give him a hug and kiss.

"Congratulations, you're the first to get hitched," Tony says.

"Thanks, Tony." I give him hugs and kisses.

"Well, tonight's your night, I don't want you walking out of here, you will need to be carried home," Mandy says.

"Keep the bubbly flowing then, my best woman."

"I will, for sure. Now mingle, it's your night."

Eighties music is playing as I walk around the bar saying hello to old friends, some I haven't seen for a very long time. The night is going great, fantastic music and bubbly flowing freely. When I mention the bar bill to Mandy, she tells me it's all sorted and not to worry. I'm sure Bradley has had some involvement in tonight.

After a few hours of dancing and drinking, my glass never seems to empty with Mandy constantly topping me up.

I see a stool empty in the bar's corner where Bradley and I first met. Taking a seat I feel very light headed as people's faces blur past me. I close my eyes briefly, and as I open them Craig is standing in front of me.

"Hello, angel, congratulations."

I feel very queasy as I try to focus on his face. His eyes cut deep into mine.

"Does the *Shag Me* offer extend to me?"

I'm frozen, his voice sending shivers down my back. Lost for words as he moves closer, his legs pushing between mine, trapping me against the wall. His hand touches my cheek as he slowly trails a single finger over my lips. "I've missed you."

The excitement and happiness I'm feeling drains from me as though a dark cloud of misery has engulfed my entire body. His hands move to my thighs. Grabbing them tight, he squeezes my legs to his body, easing me forward on the stool so I can feel his hard cock press against me. Leaning forward, he kisses me, his lips as soft and warm as I remember. I have so much Prosecco on board I take a while to react to his actions.

As he raises his hand to touch my face again, I grab his wrist tight and hold his hand away from my face.

"Don't you dare touch me again!" My words are slurred from the drink and are just a whisper, but clear enough for him to hear.

I keep a tight hold of his wrist as I stand up. "I'm not afraid of you anymore, I'm not your fucking angel either." My voice is getting louder with every word as I push him back away from me.

A shocked look spreads across his face as my anger grows, I've never had the strength to stand up to him in all our years together. I'm oblivious to the people nearby as I focus on Craig.

"You, abused me, mentally, physically, and made me feel worthless all the time we were together. You never loved me, you used me for your own satisfaction. I took a long time to recover from you and what you did. Now I have found happiness with the most wonderful man ever and you have the audacity to turn up tonight bringing your poison to the party," I shout at him the rage inside me releasing.

The music stops, and the bar falls silent as everyone turns and watches me and Craig.

"David, I'm sorry—"

"Sorry, sorry, that was your favourite word. I'm sorry, you were always sorry, Craig, until the next time and the next. Well, your words mean nothing now. You mean nothing to me, you can't hurt me anymore so get the fuck out of my face and out of my party." The word spit from my mouth in anger.

I can see the anger rising in his eyes as the words

leave my lips. That anger I have seen so many times before and I knew what was coming as he draws his fist back, ready to swing at me. Before he could move, Tony grabs his arm and spins him around.

"Want to hit someone, big man, try me."

Craig realises everyone in the bar is now staring at him. He shakes his hand free from Tony.

"He's not worth it," Craig says, glaring at me, the true man they have never seen showing through.

Mandy joins us. "You heard him, Craig, you're not welcome here."

"Okay, I'm going. I hope you can satisfy your husband better than you did me," he says, his last attempt to belittle me before turning and pushing his way through people to leave the bar.

Mandy gives me a hug. "Are you okay?" she whispers.

"Yeah, I'm fine, in fact, that felt really good to finally say that to him."

"Well, forget about him now, don't let it spoil your night. Let's have another drink."

I give her another hug. "Thanks, babes."

"What's the best woman for?"

The rest of the night goes by with no more drama and Mandy escorts me home at the end of the night. Handing me over to Bradley and apologising for my drunken state before she gets back into the taxi to take her home. He just laughs at me and helps me into the house, taking me upstairs to bed.

34

The wedding

*M*andy pins the white rose with flecks of pink to my lapel before adjusting my pink tie. I can see her eyes welling up as she smiles at me, then kisses my cheek.

"There you go, you look amazing. I'm so proud of you," she says.

I turn and face the full-length mirror in the room, the pink tie looks perfect against my white shirt, the lapels on the light grey suit framing it perfectly. My own eyes well as I look at myself, my stomach churning in knots. This is it, the day I finally become Mr. Franklin has arrived. A single tear of happiness runs down my cheek.

Mandy leans forward and wipes it off my face with her hankie. "Don't start, David, or we will both be in floods of tears before we get downstairs."

I turn and face her, my hands sweating and shaking.

I take a deep breath to control my nerves. She hugs me tight. "Are you ready?" she whispers.

"As ready as I ever will be."

There is a knock on the door, Mandy opens the door and a well-dressed young man smiles at her. "Everyone is in place, you can come down when you're ready."

"Come on, then, let's get you hitched," she says. Taking my hand, she leads me towards the door.

We only have to walk downstairs to the ceremony room, but my legs feel like jelly as we leave the room. I can feel my heart thumping heavily in my chest. I can't believe how nervous I'm feeling. As we reach the top of the stairs, a piano plays *Flashlight*, shivers run down my spine and goose bumps raise on my skin as the cello joins in. I look at Mandy, my eyes giving away my struggle to control my emotions. She squeezes my hand tightly as we walk down the stairs. They have draped pink and white roses from the handrails on the stairs, leading to flower archways spaced out across the hall to the entrance to the ceremony room. The piano and cello are still playing as we walk through the arches towards the doors to the ceremony room.

Two young men wearing top hat and tails open the doors as we approach and I catch a glimpse inside as everyone in the room stands. Mandy slips her arm around mine and gives me a kiss on the cheek. We begin walking slowly down the centre of the room. The large arch at the far end of the room is decorated in the same pink and white roses. I see Bradley for the first time, standing with his hands clasped behind his back, wearing the same grey suit as me. Danny the younger image of him by his side, he has the biggest smile across his face, as bright and glowing as his dad's. Bradley looks so handsome as he smiles at me and Mandy.

We walk slowly towards them, with the music playing in the background. It seems like the longest walk ever until I'm standing next to Bradley. My body is trembling all over as he takes my hand. I can feel him shaking as he squeezes my hand. The music stops and everyone in the room sits down. I look into Bradley's eyes and he winks at me before smiling. Taking another deep breath to calm my nerves, we turn to face each other and I feel his fingers entwine with mine. The warmth of his hands makes me feel secure. He silently mouths "I love you".

I'm startled by the woman standing in front of us as she speaks. "Welcome, family and friends of David and Bradley."

Bradley holds my hands tight as she continues.

"We are gathered here today to witness the marriage of David Harvey Wright and Bradley John Franklin. This is a day of great celebration, for a married life — a shared life is a great blessing. As David and Bradley embark on this journey together, they will be able grow together, as marriage is a garden we sow with love, and harvest in personal growth."

I can feel my legs shaking as she reads from the large silver book in her hands.

"On your journey together, the love you share must be guarded and cherished forever, for it is your most valuable treasure. Always remember these words; Love is patient and kind. Love is not jealous or boastful or proud or rude. Love never gives up, never loses faith, is always hopeful, and endures through every circumstance."

I stare deep into Bradley's eyes as her words echo around the room.

"You have written your own vows, and it is with these words you express your binding promises to love, honour, and cherish one another. If you are ready to make these promises to each other, I invite you now to read your vows. Bradley when you're ready, you may begin."

Bradley releases one of my hands and Danny hands him a white card. Coughing to clear his voice, he begins. "David, from the first moment we met, you brought a special light into my heart. You have a realistic warmth about you I have never seen in anyone before. Your wonderful smile and loving touch make me melt inside when I'm with you. I want to love and protect you every minute of every day. To show you the world and watch in wonder as you enjoy new experiences as you did on our trip to New York. I'm yours and I promise never to put anything or anyone before you in my life. You've helped me learn to love life again and to realise what joy true love brings. You are my soul mate and lover and I couldn't wish for any more. David, I love you and want you to be my husband."

I can't hold back the tears of joy as the stream down my cheeks.

"David, when you're ready you may begin."

Mandy hands me a white card and I try to hold it steady. "Bradley, you have helped me to grow when I thought there was no hope left of ever finding happiness. You have loved and supported me whenever my insecurities have got the better of me. Showing me how wonderful a man you are. You bowled me over with your love, warmth, and generosity. When I'm with you, I feel protected and so proud having you by my side. You're my world, my man, my love, and life without you would never be the same. Take my hand, my heart, my everything, as I give it all to you. Be my husband today and forever more."

"Thank you for sharing your vows with all of us. The rings you are about to place on each other's fingers are symbols of the love you expressed. They will remind you of the vows you have just spoken, and of the eternal love you have for one another. Bradley, place the ring on David's finger and repeat after me. As this ring encircles your finger… from this moment forward... so, will my love forever encircle your heart... you will never walk alone... my heart will be your shelter... my arms will be your home... I promise to do my best to love, cherish and accept you... I give you my heart until the end of time..."

My cheeks burn as Bradley repeats the words, all the time looking deep into my eyes. Once he has placed the ring fully on my finger, I repeat the same words to him. The tears filling his eyes as each word leaves my lips.

"I now pronounce you husband and husband, please take your first married kiss."

Bradley cradles my face with his hands and presses his lips to mine. The warmth engulfs me as the realisation we're married sinks in; I'm lost in his kiss. The noise of everyone clapping brings me back into the room. Bradley takes my hand and leads me back through the centre of the room to clapping and cheering of our friends.

We head outside to the gardens and pose for what seems like hundreds of photos. Once the photos are finished, we then go into the marquee for the reception dinner. Danny and Mandy both give emotional speeches before Bradley thanks everyone for coming and me for being his wonderful husband.

Everyone eats their dinner, then Danny stands up and taps his glass bringing the marquee into silence.

"I would like your attention as my dad and his wonderful husband have their first dance. Please join them."

Bradley squeezes my hand as Danny speaks, the pride glowing on his face; having his son here today has meant the world to him. He stands and pulls me to my feet leading me to the centre of the dance floor.

"This is for you, my love, a song and dance for you to remember forever more. I said the one thing I wanted to do was choose the song for our first dance. This is the first song I ever saw you dance to," he says, giving me a kiss.

The song *What is Love* plays and my thoughts go back to that very first night in the bar when I saw him sitting on the stool in the corner. This was the song that was playing as I danced out of the pub. I laugh and tears of joy overwhelm me; I'm amazed that he had remembered that moment. I wrap my arms around him as we dance to the song.

"This is where the ride of your life begins," Bradley says.

"I'm looking forward to it, my husband."

We dance and mingle for several hours until everyone's attention is caught by the sound of a helicopter landing in the grounds near the marquee.

Bradley takes my hand. "Come with me, Mr. Franklin, our carriage awaits to take us to our future."

"Where are we going?" I ask as leads me to the entrance of the marquee, all of our guests gathering to see us off.

"Remember, I said I wanted to show you the world and watch in wonder as you enjoy it."

"Yes."

"We're going on a world cruise."

I'm speechless as he leads me to the helicopter. We both wave at our guests as we climb into the seats. I kiss Bradley as the helicopter begins to leave the ground.

"I cannot believe we're going around the world." I say the shock slowly fading. "What about work, the house, my clothes?"

"Everything is sorted, welcome to your new life, Mr. Franklin," he says before leaning in to kiss me.

The End

MESSAGE FROM THE AUTHOR

David was originally written as a one-off short story, but when readers wanted more I began to explore David and Bradley's relationship in greater detail. David is close to my own heart and I feel his pain and the reason for the wall he had built to protect his emotions after his relationship with Craig.

The differences between their lives adds to the story as David experiences Bradleys lifestyle, showing how they begin to grow together draws us into their world.

Each story brings more revelations about this adorable couple and fans of the series have told me they enjoyed the regular short story updates on their lives. They are in the honeymoon period of their relationship totally in love without complications.

A massive Thank You to all my readers.

B.J

275

THANK YOU

Thank you for reading this book.

If you enjoyed it, please share with your friends as word of mouth is the greatest promoter of books. Also, if you could leave a quick review, that would be really appreciated.
B.J. SMYTH

Come and join my Facebook Readers Group BJ's Chit Chat for future book teasers, ARC opportunities, giveaways, insights into my writing and much more?

Click here for BJ's Chit Chat

Don't want to miss my next release then +follow me on my Amazon Author page - Author.to/BJ-Smyth

Printed in Poland
by Amazon Fulfillment
Poland Sp. z o.o., Wrocław

53347001R00167